Mike Carter

AF198150

Large Land

Book One: Shiv & Stitch

JustFiction Edition

Impressum/Imprint (nur für Deutschland/only for Germany)
Bibliografische Information der Deutschen Nationalbibliothek: Die Deutsche Nationalbibliothek verzeichnet diese Publikation in der Deutschen Nationalbibliografie; detaillierte bibliografische Daten sind im Internet über http://dnb.d-nb.de abrufbar.
Alle in diesem Buch genannten Marken und Produktnamen unterliegen warenzeichen-, marken- oder patentrechtlichem Schutz bzw. sind Warenzeichen oder eingetragene Warenzeichen der jeweiligen Inhaber. Die Wiedergabe von Marken, Produktnamen, Gebrauchsnamen, Handelsnamen, Warenbezeichnungen u.s.w. in diesem Werk berechtigt auch ohne besondere Kennzeichnung nicht zu der Annahme, dass solche Namen im Sinne der Warenzeichen- und Markenschutzgesetzgebung als frei zu betrachten wären und daher von jedermann benutzt werden dürften.

Coverbild: www.ingimage.com

Verlag: JustFiction! Edition ist ein Imprint der
LAP LAMBERT Academic Publishing GmbH & Co. KG
Heinrich-Böcking-Str. 6-8, 66121 Saarbrücken, Deutschland
Telefon +49 681 37 20 310, Telefax +49 681 37 20 310-9
Email: info@justfiction-edition.com

Herstellung in Deutschland:
Schaltungsdienst Lange o.H.G., Berlin
Books on Demand GmbH, Norderstedt
Reha GmbH, Saarbrücken
Amazon Distribution GmbH, Leipzig
ISBN: 978-3-8454-4588-5

Imprint (only for USA, GB)
Bibliographic information published by the Deutsche Nationalbibliothek: The Deutsche Nationalbibliothek lists this publication in the Deutsche Nationalbibliografie; detailed bibliographic data are available in the Internet at http://dnb.d-nb.de.
Any brand names and product names mentioned in this book are subject to trademark, brand or patent protection and are trademarks or registered trademarks of their respective holders. The use of brand names, product names, common names, trade names, product descriptions etc. even without a particular marking in this works is in no way to be construed to mean that such names may be regarded as unrestricted in respect of trademark and brand protection legislation and could thus be used by anyone.

Cover image: www.ingimage.com

Publisher: JustFiction! Edition
is an imprint of the publishing house
LAP LAMBERT Academic Publishing GmbH & Co. KG
Heinrich-Böcking-Str. 6-8, 66121 Saarbrücken, Germany
Phone +49 681 37 20 310, Fax +49 681 37 20 310-9
Email: info@justfiction-edition.com

Printed in the U.S.A.
Printed in the U.K. by (see last page)
ISBN: 978-3-8454-4588-5

Mike Carter

Large Land

CHAPTERS:

THE ADVENTURE
BEGINS

1

THE CUSHION CAT

"Shiv stop shoving me, ouch that was my elbow you just stood on,"

Stop complaining Stitch Come on, hurry, the others will be awake soon and there's so much to see and do."

"But Shiv are you sure it will it be alright, it's in the rules you know that we shouldn't leave the shelf, what will the others say when they find out?"

"You're not afraid are you Stitch, not afraid of what's down there on the floor?"

"Listen Shiv I may only have little legs but I'm afraid of nothing," Shiv smiled.

"Come on, I'll help you up." Shiv pulled and tugged and very soon they both stood on the polished shelf of the dresser." How do we get down there then Shiv it seems like it's a very long way."

"Look," said the knife pointing "See down there all the cracks and the knots in the wood; we can use them to climb down. Come on, the sooner we start the sooner we will get there." Taking a firm hold of the wood Shiv began carefully lowering himself over the edge of the old welsh dresser. "It's alright Stitch; if I can do it then I am sure you can."

"But Shiv we are not supposed to go on the floor." Shiv paused to look back up at him.

"It doesn't matter, no-one will find out I promise, just think of all the fun we will have before climbing back up and the others will still be fast asleep."

"It is safe isn't it?" said Stitch looking down at his friend.

"Of course it is, don't be silly. Come on we will be there before you know it."

Twizzle the ginger tomcat thought it was silly, he thought it was very silly indeed, because he had a licked clean dish and even funny shaped mice could make a nice meal. He continued to watch from his hiding place near the table. Very soon Shiv the knife and Stitch the needle reached the shiny lino. "So this is it then" said the little needle looking around."

Yes," said the knife, and it was.

3

Twizzle watched in silence as the little creatures dropped down onto the shiny lino floor.

"Mmm" he thought, "I don't remember any mice with pointy heads, and only two legs, perhaps they're from the garden, I've seen some strange things at the bottom of the garden. Still, you can't be fussy when you have a licked clean dish; I'll watch them for a little longer and see what they do. "

Twizzle gave another twitch of his long whiskers and rested his chin upon two furry paws

"What do we do now Shiv, it's very, very big down here, look, what's that over there?"

The needle started to move in the direction of an old bucket that stood by the fireplace.

"Be careful Stitch, look do you see the moving redness, can you feel the warmth? That's fire our enemy. If you venture in you will never come out." Stitch looked at him.

"It's a bit frightening down here isn't it?"

"Not as long as we are careful." They set off together across the lino and soon the needle came upon a strange looking object, Stitch gave it a little kick with his foot, "It's very soft Shiv," Shiv was smiling again.

"It's a ball of wool; have you never seen wool before stitch?"

"No, no I haven't." The little needle continued on his journey but then stopped very suddenly as he heard a voice, "It's dark, so dark, I like it when its dark whoops!" Stitch almost fell over the little black creature that stood before him. He started jumping up and down clapping his hands together "Hey look at those little legs." The beetle now began to stare at him," Let me ask you question my pointed little friend. "

"Oh yes please, go on ask me a question, I like questions go on." The beetle took a deep breath before answering, "Can you climb walls?"

"Oh that's a silly question even I wouldn't ask a silly question like that Of course I can't climb walls." The beetle smiled. "Well I can, that's why I've got lots of little legs good isn't it, see you, bye, bye." The beetle turned and disappeared beneath a dark crack in the skirting board. "Shiv, Shiv come over here, I've met a thing with lots of wall climbing legs it said: Whoops, but now it's gone." The knife had now arrived and stood beside his friend." Gone where Stitch?"

"In the wall, I mean under the wall, or was it over the wall I don't remember all I do remember is lots and lots of little legs."

"Never mind Stitch it's gone now. Come on, let's go and play on that big ginger cushion over by the table leg." The knife started to lead the way quickly followed by the needle. "Shiv I didn't know that cushions could breathe?"

"What was that Stitch?"

"Cushions, you know breathing cushions."

"Don't silly who ever heard of a breathing cushion?"

"Well I hadn't not until now but that one is breathing and it was.

~~~

Twizzle the cat who had been waiting for the right moment uncurled his long furry body and jumped to his feet then quickly began to run in the direction of Shiv and Stitch. The little needle was jumping up and down clapping his hands again he was so excited "Look Shiv a living cushion, it's a living cushion on legs and it's coming this way," Shiv began to run.

"Quickly Stitch, quickly make for that hole in the wall, hurry, hurry, that's no cushion it's a cat and a very big cat at that."

Shiv skidded to a halt on the carpet and dived into the big hole at the bottom of the skirting board. Stitch wasn't far behind as he bumped and bounced, bounced and bumped through the gap into the darkness until finally he came to rest against a cold damp pipe. "Oh let's play on the floor," he said suddenly in Shiv's direction. "Of course it's safe Stitch, you never mentioned a ginger coloured cushion with a tail and teeth did you?"

"Be quiet, look, look." They turned to see a big cat's eye staring through the hole they had just entered. "Does this mean we are in trouble Shiv?"

"I think it means we are in trouble Stitch."

~~~

Twizzle sat quietly in front of the skirting board. "Funny mice, very funny mice, I wonder if they taste differently." He continued to wait, and wait and wait. "Sooner" he purred, "Sooner or later you will have to come out and then it's going to be snip snap, Mmm, nice dinner

5

that." Back in the wall behind the skirting board Shiv and Stitch were wondering what to do. "Well we can't go out that way can we, not while the cushion cat is around?"

"Don't be silly Stitch; I told you it's not a cushion cat."

"Well you thought it was a cushion didn't you, so now it's a cushion cat."

"Look" said Shiv who had been taking a good look around "Look down there through the darkness I can see light and there's a slight breeze coming from somewhere."

"I don't care," said the needle, "It's not the same as our wooden drawer but if we have no choice I suppose we ought to go and have a look." They stood up and started to make their way along the narrow dusty passage. Occasionally they had to climb over pipes and sticking out bits of brickwork but very soon what had been a dim light became a bright light and the air was filled with the smell of flowers. "Look Stitch".

Over the last remaining pipe Shiv could see a large wide crack in the brickwork. "Look, look there's a hole leading to the outside and possible help."

"But it's a big world" said the needle. "Shiv you're not really thinking of going out there are you, not into large land, we have only ever seen it from the window."

"Stitch, the cushion cat lives on the floor. He's a big cat with big teeth; we could never cross the floor safely to the dresser, not now he knows we are here, so returning to the wooden drawer might be difficult without help."

"Well where will we get help Shiv, it's a big world out there and it might be full of more cushion cats."

The knife and the needle sat on the edge of the crack in the brickwork looking across at a waving field of green. "You can stay Stitch if you like, I will go alone and try and bring back some help, stay here in the darkness, in the dust knowing that the cat is never too far away."

"No, no Shiv I will go with you."

"Are you sure?"

"No not really but I'm coming anyway." Shiv leaned forward in the crack to get a better look at the ground below. "Look out!" cried the needle "be careful you will fall!" but it was too late. Shiv tipped forward and disappeared from sight leaving Stitch alone in the shadows. "Shiv,

6

Shiv please come back, wait for me, wait for me!" Silence, nothing but the stillness of the tunnel "Come on Shiv help me down, I'll come with you I won't be afraid I promise."

"Shut up you noisy thing, why are you shouting, you will wake my babies!" The little sparrow hopped onto a pipe next to where the needle was standing. "Babies" said Stitch "I'm not bothered about babies. What about my friend Shiv? I bet he's lying hurt and in pain on the ground, I bet he's crying but most of all I bet he's really missing me."

"Oh the knife you mean," said the sparrow?"

Of course I mean the knife, who else would I mean?"

"Well" said the sparrow, "I don't know about hurt and crying, I just saw him running as fast as his legs would carry him, down the path toward the strawberry patch."

"Running, gone without me, but I'm his best friend."

"Well he was being chased by a big ginger cat at the time. I've just seen it returning through the door into the kitchen."

"Oh I do hope Shiv is alright, tell me if I flap my arms up and down do you think I could fly down the garden?" The little sparrow laughed.

"But I'm a bird, you're not a bird, you don't have feathers."

"Yes but all you do is flap your arms up and down really quickly."

"It's not that easy my friend."

"It looks easy enough to me." He jumped out of the crack flapping his arms wildly. "Look, I can fly!" He couldn't, he fell like a stone. Did it hurt when he landed on his head? It did.

2

GHOSTS IN THE GARDEN

The little needle landed point first into the soft soil. "Help me, help me!" His legs were moving very quickly but he wasn't getting anywhere. "I told you? I said you couldn't fly."

"Why are you upside down?" said Stitch suddenly.

"Oh dear, you are silly, it's you that's upside down not me. You've landed on you head and now you're stuck fast in the soil."

"Get me out, get me out!"

"Be quiet, you'll wake the cushion cat in the cottage and we both know what that means."

"My head feels funny, Oooh, I feel dizzy." Stitch made the sparrow think of a struggling worm after new rain. "Hold tight then, I'm going to take a firm hold of your foot." The sparrow pulled and pulled with all his might and soon the needle began to rock from side to side. "Oooh please be careful I feel all dizzy again." With a sudden pop Stitch came free and landed on his knees. "Thank you, thank you. Now which way did my friend go?"

"You must travel until you see the green leaves of the strawberry patch. That's where I last saw the knife."

"Thank you, thank you." Stitch set off at a run down the long winding path. "I wish my legs were longer, I would get there a lot quicker, I'll find you Shiv, I'll find you." He ran faster and faster expecting any moment to see cushion cat following.

~~~

Back in the wooden drawer of Raven Cottage the sound of snoring filled the air. Down below on the carpet Twizzle lay looking at his dish. "Licked clean dish, pointy headed mice; it's going to be an interesting day, yes an interesting day indeed." His tail flicked lazily over his back as he turned his attention to the hole in the wall. "There's still one of you in there I know there is, but I can wait." One sleepy eye closed but the other continued to watch as he waited for his lunch a pointed lunch.

"At last" whispered Stitch "The strawberry patch" green hairy leaves on stalks waved gently in the cool breeze. "Where are you Shiv? It's me Stitch, where are you?" Before too long the needle came upon an upturned and broken plant pot. "This looks like a good place to get my breath back; I'll just pop in through the crack and rest my legs. Shiv, Shiv, it's me Stitch, where are you?" He crept into the pot and sat down in the shadows. "Shiv, Shiv!" The little voice was lifted out through the hole in the pot up and over the fruit. "Shiv it's me you friend the needle, Shiv!" Did Shiv hear him? Of course he did.

The knife had been sitting quietly under one of the big leaves munching on a strawberry when he thought he had heard a voice. He had picked himself up and started a search among the remaining plants. Then he heard it again. "Shiv, come out come out wherever you are, Shiv, Shiv!"

"Stitch I can hear you, where are you?"

"Over here Shiv, I'm underneath a plant pot, can you see it?" Shiv continued to search and then suddenly there it was over in the corner by an old spade. "I see it Stitch, I see it!" He ran the last few steps through the plants and ducked down and entered the pot.

"Oh it's so good to see you I thought the cushion cat had eaten you."

"Oh very nice I'm sure, but it was a lot worse than cushion cats I landed on my head and got stuck in the soil."

"Slow down Stitch," Shiv sat down next to this friend." Now tell me all about it".

~~~

Far, far away behind Pike Wood and past farrow field an old windmill stood deserted and empty. But deep down in the darkest part of the cellar a group of rats listened as their leader whispered instructions.

"Yes, Claw, they meet by the plum tree, you could say they will be ripe for the picking." The sound of laughing drifted up through the old wooden floor echoing round the broken staircase and escaping through a cracked window. For this was Dragon mill, lair of the Pike wood Pirates. But soon very soon silence returned and it was almost as if no one had ever been there, but of course they had.

~~~

Stitch had finished telling Shiv about his escape and now both of them were now clambering up onto the top of the plant pot. Eventually they pulled themselves over the edge then taking a deep breath looked back in the direction of the path but seeing nothing they jumped down.

"Come on Stitch we must get as far away as possible, and find somewhere safe." They pushed their way through the last few plants and stepped out onto a long green lawn. Just for a moment Stitch thought he heard water, but it was just the breeze whistling through the canes supporting some runner beans.

"Oh Shiv, it's such a long way, no cottage, no warm drawer to sleep in." The knife looked down at him.

"It's only grass Stitch and if you were just a little taller you would see what looks like a barn at the end of the orchard."

"Oh just a little taller just because you are bigger than me," he stopped to drink some of the dew that covered the bright green grass. Shiv continued to talk as he walked. "It may be a safe place to rest while we try and figure out a way back into the drawer, what do you think?" He turned, "Stitch, Stitch where are you?" Of the little needle there was no sign." You've gone and done it again haven't you." And he had.

"Shiv, Shiv quick, the little needle was out of breath.

"What's wrong Stitch, is the cushion cat in the garden?"

"Cushion cat? No, no it's worse, oh it's horrible, there are ghosts Shiv, ghosts in the garden. Come on, quickly before they see us!"

"Can't be," said the knife standing his ground, "No such thing as ghosts."

"Well these no such thing as ghosts are over there by a big glass house."

"Oh, you mean the greenhouse." "No it's not green, it's glass. There were three of them all ghostly white moving back and forward."

"Come on then Stitch, show me." They crept slowly back the way Stitch had come and there by an old rain barrel on the edge of the orchard three little white shapes moved freely over the lawn.

"Oh no look Shiv, they are coming this way!"

"Don't you think they are a little small for ghosts" said the knife starting to smile.

"Small, small, they look big to me and I've seen and heard them up close, you haven't."

"Come on Stitch," said the knife holding onto his little friend's hand, "Let's go and say hello to these ghosts of yours."

"But they don't speak they make a sort of booming noise." It wasn't long before Shiv and the frightened needle reached the crumbling brickwork of the greenhouse and there just as Stitch had said Shiv saw three ghostly shapes moving in and out of the shadows. "Hello there, I say hello can you help us?" The mysterious shapes suddenly disappeared.

"Told you so told you!" cried the needle "Horrible jumping long eared ghosts." The strange shapes reappeared near the rain barrel at the other end of the greenhouse. Shiv began dragging Stitch a little closer. "Look" said the knife laughing, "Brown and white ghosts with big pointy ears."

"Big pointy ears?" said Stitch. He looked a little harder at the three creatures that sat on the grass.

"Rabbits Stitch, they're rabbits." And they were.

~~~

The little rabbits sat upright on the lawn every now and then thumping their fluffy white tails on the ground. "Hello" said the knife "My name is Shiv and this is my best friend Stitch the needle."

One of the rabbits hopped forward its little brown nose twitching. "My name is Rosehip and back there are my brothers Briar and Nettle." The two rabbits sitting behind Rosehip gave a little wave.

"We haven't seen you on the lawn before" said the rabbit suddenly, "Are you visiting someone?"

"I fell on my head and got stuck in the ground," said Stitch smiling at the rabbits. Shiv stepped forward.

"Can you tell us anything, anything at all about the old barn over there, is it empty?"

"Oh dear no you can't go there, that's Kippers Kingdom."

"Who is Kipper then?" asked the knife turning to look at Briar and Nettle.

"Baron Kipper the spider, oh yes indeed its Kipper's Kingdom." Shiv listened in silence as the rabbit told the tale of Baron Kipper and his neighbour Compo, and of other spiders that lived in the barn, Leggy and Berry. Stitch began to fidget. "Is that it then, little incy wincey spiders, no problem?" The rabbit turned and hopped back to join the others.

"Oh of course there's Romulus of the rafters," said Nettle beginning to thump his tail a little harder. "Romulus, who's Romulus"? And what's a rafter, does it have teeth?"

"King of the garden" said Rosehip, "Anyway, we must be off, time to sleep time, to dream."

"Wait, you can't go yet you haven't told us about Romulus."

"And the rafter" said Stitch.

"Keep in the sun, you're safe in the sun, yes, yes, avoid the shadows." Without waiting for a reply the three rabbits hopped quickly away and disappeared back behind the rain barrel. "Hey wait, wait!" cried the knife, "You can't go yet, we still have questions! That's very puzzling," said Shiv.

"Well I tell you what you can be as puzzled as you like but I'm hungry." They set off together in the direction of the barn. "Never mind Shiv the barn is big and dry and very quiet but is it safe?" It wasn't.

~~~

Upriver a small group of rats gathered on the bank as they prepared for an ambush.

"I hear a new rat is in the area, and that he only has one eye." The evil looking rat with a piece missing from his tail began to gather small branches to hide the hole that the rats had dug in the path. "Rubbish, new rat, one eye indeed, I suppose he thinks he can run circles round the rest of us."

Earlobe the oldest of the rats stepped forward." Aye sounds about right, only the one eye? I suppose he will swim in circles when we make him walk the plank." The sound of their laughter drifted onto the breeze and was gone.

~~~

It had taken some time, but Shiv and Stitch finally reached the great wooden barn door.

"Shiv, what's all that yellow grass, it's everywhere?"

"Straw Stitch, now please be quiet for a little while, come on, stay in the shadows, we don't want any more surprises."

"Oh you mean I've seen a cushion cat, been dropped on my head and met a ghost surprises" Shiv smiled. "We have no choice Stitch, up there high on the beams may be the answer to all of our problems."

"Up there, up near the roof?"

"Yes look, very carefully, do you see where the two beams cross over?"

"More yellow stuff?"

"No look again." Stitch stretched himself high up on tiptoes.

"Shiv, it's a great big sticky looking very clean thing."

"Right" said the knife, "that thing is actually a web and who live on webs."

"It's not a cushion cat is it?"

"No, no try again.

Kipper, its Baron Kipper, the spider it's his home isn't it? And it was.

3

KIPPERS KINGDOM

Very high up on the beams of the old barn, Baron Kipper the spider was busy cleaning his web. "Achoo" he sneezed very loudly almost falling off, "Dust, so much dust, I really must try harder to clean my web more often." A little further along the beam Compo the spider sat very quietly in his web. "Cleaning" he muttered under his breath, "Web cleaning, if it's not that, it's all his washing strung out on a silken line. Waste of time, bound to get dirty again then he will have to start all over again." Compo reached down into one of his many pockets and pulled out a slice of very crumbly pie covered in fluff. "Mmm my favourite snack fly pie, I'm really going to enjoy this." He settled back again making himself comfortable in the centre of the web and began to eat. Meanwhile Baron Kipper had just finished the top part of his web and was working his way slowly down the silky threads. On the ends of each of his long hairy legs, little blue dusters seemed to be moving in all directions. Suddenly Baron Kipper stopped and quickly pushed all the dusters into his pockets. "Oh my I have forgotten my pie, my strawberry pie and it's still in the oven." He picked up the last duster from where it lay on the shiny web and started to hurry in the direction of the great crack in which his home was hidden.

Compo having finished his snack was busy brushing the crumbs from the fine hairs on his jumper. "I suppose I will have to go and wash my face now" he said to himself, "I really hate water." Suddenly two of the dusty strands attaching Compos web to the beam snapped. Then as the web began to sag in the middle, Compo found himself rolling head over heels over and over, eventually falling off the broken web into a large pile of flies wings and buttercup petals.

As he rolled over onto his back he disturbed a dandelion clock. Tiny seeds flew into the air covering Compo some of them even managing to get up his nose. "Oh no!" he cried loudly, "Look at this mess. My web is broken there are seeds everywhere and now I can't reach my front door, "deary me, oh deary me."

Baron Kipper who had been very busy sweeping his living room floor heard the crash putting the brush down he hurried out onto his web to see what was happening. As the spider reached the centre of his web he could just see Compo sitting up in the pile of rubbish. "Hey!" he shouted in his neighbour's direction, "Hey Compo! I warned you, this has happened before but still you refuse to clean the web."

Compo stopped brushing himself down and looked across at Baron Kipper who was sitting with a smile on his face in the middle of his nice shiny web. "Shut up Kipper, think you're clever don't you, washing this cleaning that." The spider continued to smile.

"I told you last time your web broke to clean it more often. And now look, flies wings and dandelion seeds everywhere." Baron Kipper got up and began to move back towards his front door. Compo stared after him. "Daft you are Kipper" he muttered. He brushed the last seedlings from his trousers and then with a big sigh he picked himself up, stretched himself to his full height and began to repair the damaged web.

Down below on the floor of the barn Shiv stepped out from the safety of the shadows. The little needle Stitch stood quietly behind him. "Come on," whispered the knife. They began to slowly climb up the large bales of straw that stretched ahead of them upwards and upwards towards the beam. "They don't like each other very much do they," whispered Stitch. Shiv paused and looked back, smiled at the needle, and continued to climb. Shiv reached the old oak beam first and had to wait some time before Stitch joined him. "You took your time didn't you?" he said to the needle.

"I've only got little legs you know" was the only reply. It was a very long beam and the needle and the knife were feeling very tired after the climb up the straw bales. "It's a bit dark Shiv and it's slippery too."

"Quiet" said the knife "It's only shadows from the roof. Careful now, I don't want those spiders to hear us until we learn a little more about them." They continued the journey in silence until Stitch suddenly brushed against one of the shiny new supports of Compo's web. "This is horrible!" cried the needle.

"Ssshh" said Shiv in vain as Stitch began crying for help.

"Help me, help me I'm stuck!" The more the needle struggled the worse things became.

"What's happening!" cried Compo almost falling off his web again, "Who are you, what are you doing?"

"I'm not doing anything," said Stitch still struggling, "I'm all glued up, I can't move and my legs are trapped."

Shiv slipped quietly into the shadows and watched. "I will ask you again who are you and what do you want?" Compo opened his jaws revealing two long sharp fangs.

"There are bits of food all over your teeth" said the needle, "Don't you clean them?" The spider's jaws snapped shut. "I'm Stitch the needle and I'm looking for a place to rest."

"Seems to me you are already resting on my web."

"Leave the little one alone, he doesn't mean any harm." Baron Kipper continued to move out onto his web as he spoke." Come on Compo, let him go."

"Oh no, not you again Kipper. How do I know he's not after my fly pie?"

"Fly pie?" said the needle, "Fly pie, wings, and legs and things. Give me a juicy berry anytime." Compo began to snip the strands holding Stitch to the web careful not to let the little needle see his fangs again. Suddenly with a squeal Stitch dropped from the web and rolled onto his back. Shiv stepped from the shadows. "That wasn't very nice was it? Getting my friend all glued up and then nearly dropping him on his head, do you treat all strangers the same way? We only came here for a chat."

"Ignore him," said Baron Kipper from the middle of his web, "He's not very clean and not very polite." Shiv noticed a sudden movement from the corner of his eye, he was sure it came from the straw that spilled over onto the beam. Then the others heard a sound, a rustling noise. "Look out!" cried Baron Kipper running across his web to quickly disappear behind his front door followed very quickly by Compo. A brown face full of whiskers suddenly appeared from beneath the straw and began to run in the direction of Shiv and Stitch. The needle caught a glimpse of a long brown tail before he was bowled over. "It's Monty the Mouse!" cried Compo from his hiding place.

4

TWISTED TREE

The squirrel took a step back careful to avoid the door that he had just finished painting a very bright green. He hung the tin onto a nearby branch and turned back to the small window. "Mmm, I think I will paint the frame tomorrow when I have fixed my nice new acorn knocker on the door. Those windows look a bit dirty I'll clean them now and then perhaps I will have some herb tea."

He busied himself cleaning the four little panes of glass until they sparkled in the morning sun. "That's better. Now for tea" He stepped carefully around the wet door and disappeared into the tree.

Silence returned to the branches broken only by the occasional buzzing of an insect. Overhead the sun shone brightly casting shadows on the ground beneath the squirrel's home in the twisted tree.

~~~

Back in the barn Shiv helped Stitch up from the ground where he had been accidentally knocked over by the eager mouse. "Sorry, sorry" said the mouse its whiskers twitching nervously "Little eyes you know didn't see you there in the shadows." Stitch began to brush himself down. "Yes, I know how you feel, I've only got little legs and even then sometimes they get in the way." Monty took a step towards them,

"Sorry, sorry, I was on my way to the apple store at the other end of the barn, I really must see about getting myself fixed up with some glasses."

"Do you live up here then?" said the knife looking over in the direction of the spider's web.

"No, oh my no, I only come up here for the ripe apples. I can't reach them in the orchard. No, I live by the stream in the roots of Twisted Tree. Nice and dry, a bit dark but warm. Yes, that's my home, Twisted Tree."

"Are there big holes in Twisted Tree?" asked the needle, "Big enough for us to rest in?"

Sorry, very sorry river rats' really bad lot, they have taken all the burrows. No more room, on no."

"River rats?" said Shiv suddenly looking back at the mouse, "River rats, what's a river rat?"

"Pirates" said Monty, "The forest folk call them the Pike wood Pirates. Nowhere is safe since they arrived."

"Where do they come from?" said Stitch looking around for a soft place to sit and rest his legs. Monty seemed to be thinking for a moment. "I've heard stories about them living near the haunted mill." Shiv paid more attention to what the little mouse was saying. "Dragon mill it's haunted and no-one dares to go near it anymore."

"But the river rats do" said Stitch."

"They fear nothing, nothing at all," said Monty, "And then there's the treasure, the treasure of Dragon mill."

"Where is it then this Dragon mill?" said Shiv looking for a way down off the beam even as he spoke. "Oh it's far away past Farrow Field, past Hoddle Hill towards Crag side." The mouse whiskers twitching more nervously began to move away. "Sorry I would really like to spend more time talking to you but I have to have a meal before I start back home and it's a long way for a little mouse." He waved and began silently making his way past the webs and was soon lost in shadow. "Twisted Tree I suppose we have to go there first and see if we can find out a little more about the Pike wood Pirates and the treasure."

"Go to Twisted Tree?" said Stitch, "Go to Twisted Tree, but what about the rats and water, and oh I don't feel very good about this, not very good at all."

"Come on," said the knife, "What can go wrong, after all rats are only big mice." The knife and the needle turned away from Baron Kipper's web and began the long journey back down the beam.

~~~

In the roots of Twisted Tree three large grey rats were talking in whispers. "Snake Eye knows of the treasure. He claims to have seen it in the cellars of Dragon mill." A fourth rat stepped from behind one of the many roots that cut across the large tunnel in the burrow." I am One Eye the Sly, I lead, I conquer and the treasure shall be mine." The three rats moved a little closer to the strangely dressed rat and settled down to listen.

~~~

It wasn't long before Shiv and Stitch emerged once again into the sunlight. They made their way quickly down the side of the barn and there in the distance stood Twisted Tree. "Well this is it Stitch, the sooner we reach the tree the sooner we learn more of the river rats."

"Pirates Shiv, river pirates they sound quite frightening, I feel a bit scared."

"Don't be" said the knife, "If we are careful and quiet they won't even know we've been." The little needle looked up at him. "Not know we've been, from what Monty was saying they are everywhere." They continued in silence towards the great oak tree.

~~~

Under the tree One Eye moved a little closer to the others. "Taking the treasure is easy, we wait until the other rats have gone then we take over. We move everyone into Dragon mill and defend it from strength. There are far more of us than them." The rats continued to make plans to conquer Dragon mill.

~~~

"There it is, look Shiv, it's there   I can see lots and lots of roots now." Twisted tree rose high up into the sky, Shiv and Stitch couldn't even see the top branches. They quickly ran from bush to bush making use of all the natural places to hide. "It's very quiet," said the needle "Nothing much seems to be happening."

"Yes but we must be careful we've been fooled before remember, anyway the rats are supposed to be in tunnels beneath the tree."

"Look Shiv, something's coming out from a burrow." They stood silently as an evil looking grey rat tucked something down into his pocket and disappeared from sight around the back of the tree. Shiv though he heard a splashing sound, but then nothing. "Not very nice looking are they Stitch."

"No they have long teeth, long claws and long legs."

"And they are big Stitch, very big; I wouldn't like to tangle with them."

"Look Shiv, what's that? It's moving I'm sure it moved. "And something was on the move in a small clump of grass ahead of them. "It's not moving very quickly is it?"

"Do you mind, we never move quickly, everyone knows that."

"Known for what?" said the needle.

"Not moving very quickly of course."

"What's that strange looking thing you are carrying around? It looks very heavy. Is that why you move so slowly?" The garden snail decided he had seen and heard enough from the strange pointed creature and tucked himself back into his shell." Look Shiv, look, he's carrying his house around on his back." And he was.

~~~

Deep down deep in a burrow beneath Twisted Tree the rats were almost ready to leave. "We shall meet up again by the bushes at the end of Farrow Field. Spread the word to our friends on the riverbank, and make sure that our friends at Bracken Mill are told. Now, let's pack up in preparation for the journey. There's food over in the far corner of the tunnel. It was left by the rabbits that we scared away when we moved in."

The rats scurried around the burrow gathering together all the food and weapons. "One of you must prepare to seal the entrance when we leave. Twigs and leaves have been prepared. Come on, hurry

~~~

"The drawer was never like this was it Shiv?"

"What you really mean is same old friends, same old games that was boring."

"Yes, but safe Shiv very comfortable and very safe."

"Look Stitch, at last we have arrived." They climbed over the long twisted roots that spread away from the trunk and from which the tree had been given its name. "This is hard work," said the little needle climbing from one root to another, who was not really sure what he was supposed to be looking for. "Quiet Stitch, there are river rats around here somewhere."

~~~

Not far away was the stream and from a hiding place among a small patch of bulrushes twelve trees the toad watched as Shiv and Stitch picked their way over the roots at the base of the tree. "What curious little things they are" he murmured, "thin and long and pointed, very, very strange." His tongue suddenly appeared from his mouth as he aimed at a passing insect. "Mmm, nice, now what are they doing?"

~~~

"Stitch listen, Voices, I can hear voices, they are coming from somewhere below us."

"Yes, I hear them Shiv, I'm sure they are over that way a bit." There was a sudden movement beneath his feet then the ground opened up before him. "Help me help!" Stitch rolled over and over, banging and bumping his head as he tumbled down the hidden tunnel, he came to rest on a pile of small twigs and leaves. "Welcome pointy, welcome to the world of One Eye the Sly, are you afraid?" He was.

5

ONE EYE THE SLY

Stitch was as comfortable as he could be on the dry soil and was staring into the shadows; he could just see the entrance of the small tunnel in which One Eye had trapped him he began to worry, he knew that Shiv would be unable to get past the rats. There were still two of them there and with those big teeth and sharp claws they would easily beat the knife. The little needle reached into his pocket for the very last piece of blackberry and settled back to wait and see what would happen.

~~~

Meanwhile by a rusting plough on the edge of the field just a short distance from Twisted Tree, Shiv was thinking. He knew that the rescue of his friend on his own was not possible, and he was going to need help. His thoughts returned to all his other friends in Raven Cottage. But the Cushion Cat had made sure that he could not be returning there for some time. Briar, Rosehip and Nettle were no match for the river rats and Baron Kipper was too small. He settled down into the shade feeling the warmth of the metal against his back. "If only I was somewhere else where there were no river rats, if only I was back in the drawer in Raven Cottage I would sleep." His eyes began to slowly close and he even managed a little yawn. "There must be a way, I must rescue Stitch soon. If they take him to Dragon mill escape will be impossible." He settled back and very soon his head began to nod. The gentle sound of snoring was lifted and carried away on the breeze.

~~~

Back in the tunnel the little needle began picking at the soil. "I know, I can dig a tunnel," he murmured to himself. But Stitch knew that somewhere very close by was the stream. What if water was to leak into the tunnel, after all he couldn't swim. His thoughts were broken by the appearance of Reb. "Hey you small thin pointy thing."

"Stitch is my name."

"Yes, yes. Come on pointy thing, come with me." Stitch stood up and followed the evil looking rat into the main tunnel. "Ahhhh so there you are." One Eye the Sly moved towards the needle. "Well I wasn't going anywhere was I? I mean, I'm not a mole, or a worm and you can't dig very well when you're small."

22

"Silence" The time has come for our journey to Dragon mill, you can forget your friends, forget Raven Cottage. You're a guest of the Pike wood Pirates." The one-eyed rat began to laugh, and laugh.

~~~

In the field Shiv opened his eyes, "Stitch" The single word escaped from his lips. He stood up and brushed himself down. "There must be someone who can help. I would do anything for some help right now."

"Anything, you would do anything?" The voice was very deep and took Shiv by surprise. He tried quickly to step back into the shadows. "Who are you? Where are you? Show yourself." A large head suddenly thrust itself out of the bramble just to his left.

"Hello, here I am, Fleet foot Fang" he laughed. "Funny, that almost rhymed. Don't meet many poetic foxes do you? I roar, I eat, and my coat is neat" the fox began to laugh again. "Stop it, stop it!" cried Shiv angrily "My friend is a prisoner of the river rats and all you can do is laugh." A deep growl came from the fox's throat and Shiv could see a long red tongue firmly trapped behind some very sharp teeth. "River rats, no doubt you speak of One Eye the Sly and his friends, if you need help you shall have help my strange looking friend. By what name do you go?"

"I'm Shiv the knife and we don't have too much time." The fox started to grin just a little. Then his deep throaty laugh got louder. "Come on then Shiv the knife, up on my back, let's rescue this friend of yours. Tally ho as my enemies say." The fox and the knife moved away from the plough in the direction of Twisted Tree.

~~~

One Eye the sly finished packing the small knapsack and pushed it roughly in the needles direction. "Come on thin pointy thing that's food for the journey, you very lucky that I'm a generous rat," he started to laugh. "In fact you could say I'm generous to a point." He pushed the needle in the direction of the circle of sunlight that bathed the burrows entrance. "Take firm hold of that knapsack, it's the last food you will see for a while. Reb, conceal the entrance, we don't want anyone else finding it do we?" The evil looking rat moved off to gather up the leaves and sticks to block the entrance once they had emerged from below the roots of Twisted Tree.

23

"How do we travel then?" said Stitch "It's a long way to Dragon mill, further than pike wood and Farrow Field."

"Mmmm curious little thing aren't you? Well pointy, we travel by river, by river and boat."

"Water, water but I can't swim, not with my little legs, I can't!" One Eye the sly threw back his head and began to laugh, the three of them emerged out of the burrow and into the midday sun. One Eye paused for a moment to look carefully over the top of the tangled roots. "All clear Reb, bring him round here and keep him quiet, I will prepare the boat."

~~~

Fang and Shiv watched silently from their hiding place on the bank of the stream "They are coming out," said the knife "Three of them I think."

"Yes, I fancy one of them is the sly one, look, see the rat with the patch over his eye and thorn tucked in his belt, that's One Eye the Sly."

"They are moving round to the back of the tree. Come on Fang."

"Steady my friend, steady, come now, climb on my shoulders, it's time to give these river rats a big surprise. Now when I give the word you shout as loud as you possibly can. With any luck we can take them completely by surprise."

Shiv climbed up onto the fox's broad shoulders. "Ready?" said Fang

"Ready," said the knife.

"Tally ho!" "Now Shiv, now" "Tally ho, tally ho!"

~~~

One Eye the Sly had just finished untying the small rowing boat that floated unseen beneath one of the large roots that disappeared beneath the water of the stream. "Quickly now Reb, we have a long journey ahead of us." Reb the rat pushed the needle firmly in the back. "Move pointy thing; go on, little legs or not one way or another you're getting into that boat." Suddenly the air was filled with a horrible noise.

"Look out One Eye its Fang and there's someone with him."

"Tally ho; tally ho, down with the Pike wood Pirates." The fox leapt over the first few twisted roots making straight for the rat. "Jump Shiv now" The knife stood up holding tightly onto *one of Fang's ears and then at the right moment leapt into the air. Over and over he tumbled, landing with a crunch on the back of a very surprised rat. Reb fell forward banging his nose on his rucksack. "Get up, get up, we need to launch the boat, hurry, hurry."*

In all the confusion Shiv ran directly to his friend the needle who continued to look around for a way to escape. "Hurry Reb" One Eye pulled and tugged at the boat until finally it floated free of its hiding place. With one mighty leap One Eye landed on the boat and reached for the fallen oars. Reb picked himself up and with a squeal of fear jumped clear over the shoulders of Shiv and Stitch to land half in and half out of the boat. He hurriedly pulled himself aboard. "Row One Eye, row," he felt the large bump that had appeared right on the top of his head. "Tally ho!" The fox front paws now submerged in the water reached forward and with one snap of his jaws lifted the wooden boat high into the air. He shook it and shook it, small pieces falling among the roots.

~~~

"Help, help!" one Eye and Reb fell from the crushed boat into the stream and began to swim stopping only to look back to see the last pieces of the boat dropping from the fox's jaws onto the river bank.

"One day Fang, one day, come on Reb, swim." And they did.

<u>6</u>

A STITCH IN TIME

The knife and the needle sat relaxing on the roots of Twisted Tree watching Reb and One Eye swim into the distance. The last pieces of the boat had now sunk beneath the stream and Fang was removing the fragments of wood from his teeth. "It was horrible Shiv they kept me in a dark tunnel all alone. I was really frightened."

"It's over Stitch the river rats have been defeated for now and soon it will be time to move on." Then it was Fangs turn to speak.

"Just a moment my little friend, you owe me a debt, but now is not the time for repayment but one day soon I will call upon you again, I have an old score to settle with my enemy White Wing. Anyway, more of that another day it's time I made my way to the chicken coop."

"Chicken coop" said the needle "Why a chicken coop?"

"Dinner my friend, a feathery dinner," the fox laughed and with a final wave began to run downstream until finally even his bushy tail was hidden in the hedgerows. "I've got some food Shiv it was given to me by One Eye for the journey." They opened up the rucksack and then sat back to eat a well-deserved meal. The sun was hot and very soon the memory of the river rats began to fade into the shadows.

~~~

"Dig, dig, dig, dig deep down in the dark, searching out a juicy worm whose life will soon depart." Suddenly the mole stopped singing, as his nose broke clear of the crumbly earth. "Oooh the sun is bright today, I don't like bright sun, I don't like it at all, yes I prefer a drop of rain any day." He brushed the soil from his paws and took a good look around. He couldn't see very much because he couldn't see very far. "It seems very quiet I'll just stretch out in the shade of that branch for a little while before I continue my search." Short Tail the mole scurried across the piece of ground that separated him from his tunnel and the branch, and safely made his way into the shadows. "That's better, no sun in here, now for a rest." The mole stepped into the hidden loop of thin wire and with another step it closed tightly around his foot. "Help, help I'm trapped!" And he was.

~~~

Come on Stitch, time we were on the move." Shiv stood up brushing the crumbs from his jumper.

"Where" said the needle, "Where shall we go?"

"Downstream Stitch, there is no other way. It's impossible to cross the water here and anyway the further we are from Twisted Tree the better." By now the little needle was on his feet hands in his pockets. "Stay close to the hedgerow and bushes. The less we are seen on our journey the more chance we have of succeeding." They both stepped carefully over the tree's roots and set off in the direction of the hedgerow. "Do you think we will meet the river rats again? I didn't like that One Eye the Sly." Shiv thought for a moment.

"Well Stitch I know it isn't what you want to hear but I have a feeling that our paths may cross again one day." They continued on and very soon disappeared into the cool shade of the hedgerow silence returned to Twisted Tree. There was nothing now but the hum of insects high in the branches.

From his concealed hiding place in the bulrushes Twelve Trees the toad looked out. "Mmm, I think I will keep an eye on those two little strangers, yes, yes I will." With a plop he disappeared beneath the rippling water.

~~~

The more Short Tail pulled the tighter the snare became, he pulled and tugged and tugged and pulled and very soon was out of breath. He knew that this was something to do with the land giants; he had lost friends in the past never to be seen again. "Oh dear, oh dear, what am I going to do?" He stopped tugging for a moment and sat back out of breath. "Darkness will bring the land giants, but none of my friends pass this way, it's too close to the water of the river rats, no one will come, oh dear, oh dear."

~~~

Stitch stumbled just managing not to fall. "Shiv, Shiv slow down, what about my little legs?" The knife slowed a little as he continued to make his way through the darkness of the hedgerow. "Ouch, ouch, my foot" Shiv turned to see Stitch jumping from one leg to another. "I've been bitten on my foot. It's a rat, it's a river rat!"

"No it's not, my name is Snuffle the hedgehog and that's my head you are standing on."

"Oh so sorry," said Stitch hopping to one side as he held tightly to his injured foot. " Have to be very careful you know my legs are so little sometimes I can hardly see them at all that's probably why I stood on your head. "But it's not really my fault what are you doing hiding beneath all those leaves in the middle of the day?" Snuffle looked at the little needle. "Sleeping of course, don't you know that hedgehogs sleep when the sun is high? And anyway, we don't expect strange looking creatures like you in the hedgerow." Shiv took a step forward. "I apologise on behalf of my friend and myself. We didn't realise that your bed was hidden beneath the leaves."

"Very well then" said the hedgehog, "But you really must be more careful where you put your feet in the future. Now if you don't mind I'm going to go back to sleep." Shiv and Stitch took a last look at Snuffle and set off once more into the hedgerow. "Funny place to sleep right in the middle of a hedge but I did like him," "why is that?" said the knife. "Didn't you see he only had little legs?" Shiv laughed and continued on his way. "Little legs" though Stitch, "He only had little legs, just like me." He smiled and continued to walk. Short Tail having rested was trying to bite through the snare that held his foot firmly in its grip. "Oh this is bad it's too hard and the peg is too deep. I'll have to shout for help and hope, that someone hears me. Help me, help me!" In the hedgerow Shiv stopped suddenly.

"Stitch, listen, do you hear that?"

"Hear what?" said the needle still limping a little from his meeting with the hedgehog. "Listen, listen." Stitch strained his ears and then there it was a voice somewhere outside of the hedgerow. A voice shouting for help "I hear it Shiv, I hear it," "come on, let's go and look." High in the trunk of Dead Tree another was woken from his sleep. A large brown white head turned first to the left and then to the right. Romulus stretched himself and revealed his talons. "Food" he yawned, "unusual but welcome now where is that voice coming from?" The barn owl stepped sleepily from the hollow of the tree and began to search. "The stream, no it's not coming from that direction." His ears continued to twitch fine tuning all the time, "Got you." His eyes came to rest upon the fallen branch by the hedgerow." It's hunting time." And it was.

~~~

The little needle and the knife crept from their hiding place beneath the hedgerow and stood listening. "It's over there Shiv by that fallen branch. I can hear the voice coming from over there." Before Shiv could even reply the needle began to limp very quickly across the open ground in the direction of the old branch. "Here I come. Don't worry, I'll help you." Stitch reached the branch just as a dark shadow seemed to fill the whole sky. "Look out! Look out, it's Romulus!" The little voice seemed to be coming from beneath the wood. Stitch looked up to see a really big beak only inches away from his head. He dropped quickly to the floor as the owl's talons caught the material on the sleeve of his coat. "In here, in here!" The needle stood up and limped into the shadows beneath the branch. "That was close," said Stitch bravely, now why all the shouting?" Short Tail pointed to his foot.

"It's a land giant trap; I didn't see it in the darkness." The needle stepped forward to get a better look.

"Oh that's not very nice is it, how can I help?"

"The knot is too small for my claws, do you think you could try and loosen it?" As Stitch began to work on the knot securing the snare he told Short Tail about his adventures. He spoke of the cushion car at Raven Cottage, and of mice, spiders and even rats. "Oh dear, oh dear, you have had some trouble, but I think I know someone who can help." There was a sudden noise close to the branch and in popped Shiv breathing heavily and very red in the face. "So that was Romulus he gave me a real fright but I think he's given up all thoughts of food. I saw him disappearing into a hole in that dead tree."

"Glad you're safe Shiv," with a final tug the snare came free from the moles foot. "This is Short Tail he was taking a rest from tunnelling, and thought it was safe."

"Seems that nowhere is safe in big world" said the knife sitting down, "now which way do we go from here?"

"I was trying to tell your little friend I know someone who may be able to help." Shiv and Stitch settled back and listened carefully to Short Tail's story.

Unseen by the three Saw tooth the weasel lay very quietly on top of the log. Was he listening?

Oh course he was.

7

TWELVE TREES

Twelve trees the toad sat on the edge of the lily leaf surrounded by his friends. "Quiet now quiet, I have been watching the little strangers very carefully. They show courage, but the time is coming when they will need our help."

"Why should we?" said croak and unfriendly frog.

"Simple really croak, in return for our help they may be able to help us."

"Help why do we need help, we are better off without them?"

"I'm sure you haven't forgotten Rush already?"

"You're talking about the Polo the Pike how can they help us to get rid of him?" Twelve trees took a good look around. "I have a plan my friends, a plan that will rid us of Polo forever. But for now we must watch the pointed ones carefully for soon they will arrive at Cowslip Copse and you all know what that means."

"Stinger"

"Yes croak Stinger the stoat we must prepare." The frogs and toads plopped into the water one by one and began to swim.

~ ~ ~

"A dog" said Stitch, "A great big dog with great big teeth, that's worse than cushion cats." Short Tail stared at the little needle. "Cats don't like dogs, dogs don't like cats. Dogs and cats are trouble and while there's trouble you can slip back into the drawer in Raven Cottage."

"Great idea" said Shiv feeling better already, "Where is this dog. Where does it live?"

"His name is here boy and he lives on the edge of Pike wood, the other side of the stream."

"The other side of the stream I'm just a little needle who cannot swim, and that's a big stream. The only boat I have ever seen now lies in pieces at the bottom of that stream, cross the stream indeed." Shiv the knife suddenly jumped to his feet.

"Enough of this Stitch it's something for us to think about."

"Yes and that's all I'm going to do, think about it." The needle turned back to Short Tail.

"Glad I could help I think it's safe to go back to your tunnel now we will keep watch." The knife and the needle shook hands with the mole and watched him hurry back to his hole. With a final wave he disappeared beneath the ground. "Come on then Stitch, it's time we were moving on." The two friends set off back in the direction of the hedgerow to continue their journey.

On top of the branch Saw tooth lifted himself up from his hiding place. "So you have decided to continue with your journey, I must go ahead and warn Stinger."

~ ~ ~

It wasn't too long before Shiv and Stitch reached the very end of the hedgerow. They stepped out very carefully making sure to stay in the shadows. "Look, look Shiv up ahead." Across the open piece of ground they could see a lot of bushes with a big wooden gate in the middle, "Shiv why would someone put a gate on some bushes?"

"I don't know," said the knife, "But we are going to find out. Come on, quickly run to the first fence post and then carefully follow the posts." The needle and the knife dashed across the open ground and soon reached the safety of the rusty old barbed wire fence. "Come on Stitch. Down to the next post," they began slowly to make their way along the old fence that separated the field from the stream.

~ ~ ~

Stinger, Saw tooth and Squint were looking through the bars of the wooden gate behind the old well in Cowslip Copse, they watched as the two strange little creatures ran quickly along the fence towards them. "Well done saw tooth you was right to tell me about them." Saw tooth nodded. "Come little pointed ones," said Squint licking his lips, "its dinner time and there are three hungry mouths to feed." He laughed quietly and went back to watching events through the wooden gate.

~ ~ ~

"My feet are sore Shiv. I've walked such a long way could we rest for a little while." Shiv turned back to his friend the needle. "I do understand Stitch about having little legs, and having to walk twice as far as me, but it's dangerous out here nothing ever seems to be what it appears to be. And yes, my legs grow weary too but soon the sun will be leaving the sky and there will be no safety in darkness." The little needle looked up at him.

"I suppose that means no, it's a lot easier to say no Shiv, no rest, instead of going on and on and on."

"Come on then, two more posts and we will reach the edge of the bushes. It's got to be better than being stuck out here." Shiv and Stitch continued their journey.

~~~

Stinger jumped down from his hiding place on the back of the crumbling old well. "Come on you two, up to the gate, they will be here soon." The stoats and the weasels moved silently into position behind the old wooden gate. "Come on" whispered Stinger, "Please, please when you reach the last post turn this way." And of course they did.

~~~

"Shiv listen, did you hear that?" The knife stopped and turned.

"All I can hear stitch, is the sound of the stream nearby."

"Well I thought just for a moment that I heard laughter somewhere up there just ahead of us."

"Sorry Stitch I didn't hear anything like that, darkness will be with us soon, we must hurry." The knife continued to make his way along the side of the bushes. Stitch began to whisper to himself "I wonder what our friends from the drawer are doing I wonder if they miss us at all?"

"Did you say something Stitch?"

"No Shiv, it was nothing, nothing, oh wait a minute there was one thing."

"What's that?" "If I have to go to so much trouble with two little legs, I wonder what it must be like for Snuffle after all he has four." Shiv began to smile.

~~~

"You have a plan then Stinger?"

"Yes I think the best thing to do is too bite them you know on their legs, that way they won't be able to run and we can eat them whenever we are ready."

"Mmm food, I am hungry very hungry, I can hardly wait."

"Shhh here they come." Stinger, Saw tooth and Squint settled back to wait.

~~~

"Hey you, you over there, I wouldn't do that if I was you." Stitch almost fell over as a large toad hopped from behind a rock "Wouldn't do what?" said the knife.

"Continue of your journey of course. There is evil waiting for you near the gate and evil wears a very big smile full of teeth, three sets of teeth to be exact."

The knife took a step back. "Rats?"

"No not river rats, weasels and stoats this is their kingdom, and they don't take very kindly to strangers.

"If they don't take kindly what do they do then?" said Stitch.

"Eat them of course," replied the toad. The knife moved a little closer and began to speak in whispers. "If we can't go forward and we can't go back because there's danger from Romulus, what can we do?"

"Why cross the stream of course, continue you journey on the far bank safe from Stinger and his band."

"Anyway" said the needle looking into the great big eyes of the creature, "Who are you?"

"Forgive me I forgot to introduce myself, I am twelve trees the toad, your friend, and a friend in need is a friend indeed."

"Do you need help then?" said the needle. Twelve trees began to smile.

"Well yes I do but we can talk about that later come with me. Quickly now, we must reach the stream before Stinger realises what is happening come on," cried twelve trees taking great big leaps as he hopped back in the direction of the stream. "All right for him, look at his legs Shiv; they're even bigger than you, I bet you can't hop."

"Stitch, save your energy for running, if the stoats and weasels realise what's happened they will be upon us in no time."

"I wish I could hop," said the needle, "If I could hop on my legs I wouldn't have to walk so far would I?"

"Come on you two hurry, hurry. It's not very far now."

"No but far enough." Stinger leapt from the bush in front of them baring his teeth.

"Thought you would make it and get clean away did you? Not much chance of that, after all I cannot have you cheat me of a meal, that wouldn't be very nice. Squint and Saw tooth will be here soon, then you can say goodbye to each other because you are both on the menu."

"Foxes come and foxes go but only Fang shouts Tally ho!" The fox had appeared from the long barley growing in the field. Head held high, bushy tail upright he leapt straight at Stinger. *"Look out Stinger, here I come you're reign of evil, it is done Tally ho!"*

"Doesn't he make a lot of noise" said the needle, *"It's a wonder he ever catches any food, he's always shouting that silly tally ho everywhere."*

"But he is good isn't he Stitch?"

"Yes he's very good hey I wonder if he can hop." Fang caught Stinger by the tail and lifted him high into the air and began swinging the Stoat from side to side before releasing him. The stoat tumbled head over heels up and over the bush to disappear from sight. *"Stingers flown up oh so high, he won't be back I wonder why, "the fox waved his bushy tail. "Now for the others come out come out wherever you are."* The fox sprang forward only to return from the bush with a weasel handing from his mouth. *"Oh you smell,"* said Fang between clenched teeth, *"Had a bath recently?"* Before waiting for a reply he threw the struggling weasel into the nearby stream. Stitch watched as it landed with a splash and began quickly swimming for the bank, where he watched it crawl out and disappear into the bracken. *"This is fun,"* said the fox, *"Two down, and one to go".* Squint jumped from his hiding place, grabbed Stitch by the arm and began to run. Twelve trees saw what was happening and shouted a warning. *"Look out! Look out, he has Stitch!*

8

THE GOOD SHIP BULRUSH

The evil looking weasel Squint with Stitch held in his jaws tried really hard to pass the fox that was now blocking his escape. Then suddenly he saw an opening, it was difficult but with a final squeeze he managed to scrape between Fang and the bush, but oh too late he realised his mistake. He had the stream in front of him and now the fox behind; there could be no escape now. He quickly ran to the streams edge and began making his way over on to a log, "keep back, please back." The fox approached the edge of the stream silently. Squint took a step back in fright, his left leg now knee deep in water. "Oh what am I going to do now"? Fang growled,

"You may well have the needle but I have you." The fox continued to watch from the bank as the weasel looked from left to right and back again. "Release him Squint and I'll let you go."

"No, no I don't trust you, you'll eat me." "Fang roared with laughter.

"Eat you I don't think so my smelly little friend you wouldn't taste the same."

"Taste the same, oh dear the same as what?"

"Fur and feathers, that's a chicken to you, different oh yes, give me a nice juicy chicken any day."

~~~

Unseen by the weasel and the fox a long row of silver bubbles suddenly appeared a small distance away from where the weasel was trying to keep his balance on the log. Then without warning there was a sudden movement in the water, the weasel jumped clear off the log, dropping Stitch into the water as he did so. "Ouch, ouch, get it off, get it off! Oh please, please get it off." Polo the Pike was holding on to the weasel's leg, the big pike leapt clear out of the water. "Ouch, ouch" The weasel danced and jumped, jumped and danced. Polo suddenly realising that the weasel was proving too much of a challenge let go and dropped back into the stream, a little row of bubbles appeared and then disappeared into the distance.

Squint now hopping from one leg to another suddenly saw his chance and in all the confusion leapt into the water and began to swim as fast as he could upstream. "That's the last we shall see of him for a while." Said the grinning fox,

"Yes, yes that's terrific, but Stitch where's Stitch?" The knife and the fox stood on the edge of the stream searching for the little needle, but could see nothing just the weasel who was almost out of sight. No bubbles, no nothing, no Stitch. "He's gone!" cried Shiv suddenly, "My best friend's gone forever."

"Fear not my friend, we will find him." Twelve trees hopped into the stream and with a splash began to swim. Shiv stood silently watching as the toad got further and further away. "I am sorry your friend is missing Shiv," said the fox, placing a furry paw on Shiv's shoulder, "I like the little pointy one. I hope you are successful in your search but there is no more I can do here; I must get back to my home. I must return to the hunt so that I may feed my family."

"Family?" said the knife, "You never mentioned family."

"All in good time" said the fox, "I have a feeling that our paths will cross again. Farewell brave Shiv, I wish you well." Fang turned away and was soon lost among the waving barley. "Stitch, Stitch where are you? Don't leave me alone in big world. It's a strange, frightening place. Stitch, Stitch, please come back. Shiv's voice echoed across the emptiness of the stream. "I shall miss you and yes I shall miss your little legs." He continued to shout for a while and then as the shadows of the day began to lengthen he sat down upon the bank and closed his eyes.

~~~

Hidden in the shadows of Dragon mill One Eye the Sly gathered his Pike wood pirates around him. "Trouble" he said speaking to the group of strange looking rats, "The pointy things are becoming a threat to everything we stand for, somehow we must capture them."

"Well how will we do that they have that big furry fox as a friend now?"

"Yes please tell us how it will be done."

"The tall one Shiv is a curious creature even now I think he is making his way here to Dragon mill, after all he has been told about the treasure I am sure of that."

"Aye the treasure of Dragon mill little does the pointy one realise what lies ahead of him."
The sound of laughter was lifted high up into the rafters to be lost in the darkness.

~~~

Shiv was dreaming of the great fire in the kitchen, Stitch was just buttering some freshly
made toast, and there was homemade jam, and tasty cheese. "Shiv, Shiv wake up, please
wake up," the image of Raven Cottage quickly disappeared to be replaced by the sound of
slow running water of the stream. "Come on Shiv, we've found him, we've found Stitch."
Shiv was now wide awake he stood up quickly and looked around. Twelve trees sat quietly
on a large leaf in the middle of the stream. "Come on, come on." Shiv wasn't quite sure why
but something just didn't seem right. "Come on pointy, come on." Then Shiv noticed
something half sunken in the stream, it was very close to the leaf, and it was very close to
twelve trees, "It's a rat!" he screamed. With a mighty leap twelve trees left the lily pad just as
the evil looking rat pushed a large thorn through it. "Shiv, are you the one known as Shiv? I
have a message here for the pointy one."

"Well here I am." Shiv moved a little closer to the bank. The rat was studying him.

"Oh yes, yes I see now what he meant."

"What who meant?" asked the knife.

"Never mind I have a message and a warning beware of the mill never venture near Dragon
mill if you value your life and the life of your friend."

"Really and who may I ask sends such a strange message?"

"One Eye the Sly of course, you must stay away from dragon mill and the treasure that lies
hidden within the darkness. The mill is the home of the Pike wood Pirates."

"Pirates what are you talking about?"

"Oh forget it, they didn't tell me that delivering this message would be such hard work. As if
swimming all this way wasn't bad enough. I have had enough now, Pirates, private property
keep out, and big bites for trespassers okay do you understand now, do you?"

"Yes I think so, well thanks for the message, oh before you go I have one for this one eyed
boss of yours."

"What is it?" said the rat, getting ready to leave.

"Pike wood Pirates of not you should stay well away from me."

"And me of course," Shiv turned to see his friend being helped onto the bank. He began to laugh and clap his hands. "Yes tell your boss, Shiv and Stitch are here to stay."

"Shiny points, nasty rats, swallowing dirty river water I will be ill I know I will. And now another long swim upstream and for what a pat on the back?" The rat sank beneath the water and was gone.

There was much laughter as Stitch explained how he came to be rescued from the stream. He told Shiv how he had bobbed up and down in the water hitting the bottom a few times before being found by Trig, who brought him onto the bank further downstream. He also told Shiv of something strange he had seen in the bulrushes. "It was a strange boat with a funny front bit perhaps we will be able to use it to carry on our journey as we search for a new home?" Shiv and Stitch sat down beside the fire where they were joined by twelve trees and his friends. "Nettle tea everybody." Newt filled up the little acorn cups with hot nettle tea as together they all watched the sun begin to set.

~~~

"What do you mean they are here to stay"? One Eye the Sly took hold of the rat by the collar and began to shake him. "Stay, stay, I'm not having that oh no stay not a chance." The poor tired rat began to cough. "I'm sorry One Eye, there was so many of them they were everywhere, but I almost wounded twelve trees."

"So much for surprise" snarled One Eye, "Are you sure that pointy said he was staying?"

"Yes, yes One Eye he did and that other small one the needle I think his name is Stitchy or something like that. I think they are coming after the treasure."

"Well first things first its Stitch not Stitchy, and the treasure is going nowhere we will make sure of that. " One Eye pushed the rat to one side, "Let them come, we will have a surprise waiting for them. No-one has ever frightened the Pike wood Pirates; well not while I have been the leader." The river rats moved in single file towards the old paddle wheel. It wasn't long before silence returned to the mill.

~~~

As darkness began to fall across the land Shiv and Stitch having now finished their nettle tea were very carefully carried across the stream by twelve trees and friends. "This is as far as we go I'm afraid. The land past the bulrush is claimed by others of our kind, we wish you luck on your journey." Shiv and Stitch shook hands with the friendly toad and with a last wave to the others set off in the direction of the bulrushes and the strange boat that Stitch had seen. "Look Shiv look, there it is." Bobbing gently up and down on the water trapped by the bulrushes was a kettle. It was blackened and dented and most of its spout was missing. "It's a kettle Stitch, a broken kettle."

"Yes, yes," murmured the needle, "But it's floating and it's dry."

"Of course your right" said the knife, "Well you found it so you shall name it."

"Name oh can I really, oh good then we shall call it Bulrush, the good ship Bulrush."

"I like it Stitch, it's a good name, come on, and we will collect grass and berries for the journey."

"Grass Shiv, grass, I don't eat grass, cows eat grass I don't like the taste."

"Really Stitch it's not for eating it will make a nice soft bed." They busied themselves loading up the little kettle and in no time at all they were ready to continue their journey.

~~~

From his hiding place on the bank Stinger the stoat was deep in thought. Suddenly he began to whisper. "So you travel the stream by boat that means by morning you will reach Bracken Weir, Mmm." The stoat continued to watch from the bank.

~~~

"This is it Stitch, come on I'll help you." Shiv lifted the little needle over the edge of the kettle, and then giving their new home a final push jumped up onto the spout and scrambled inside. The kettle moved slowly along the stream catching the current, and began spinning gently away from the bulrushes. Shiv climbed up and looked over the kettle's edge and very soon after a struggle Stitch joined him. "Look" said the little needle, "There's the tree and can it be yes its Raven Cottage."

~~~

On the bank Stinger continued to watch from his hiding place. "See you at Bracken Weir pointy." He slipped back in to the undergrowth and was gone.

Back in the kettle the needle was tucking into one of the berries. "Will we ever go home Shiv?"

"Of course" said the knife, "One day, one day soon"

"Oh and Shiv just one more thing I need to ask?"

"Yes?" said the knife looking over at his friend.

"Will it happen one day?"

"Will what happen?"

"Will my legs grow bigger?" They both laughed and laughed and soon they were gone.

9

BRACKEN WEIR

Tik Tak was having a bad day he seemed to have had a lot of bad days. Three young crows that lived in a tree on the edge of Farrow Field were playfully pulling at the straw sticking out from the scarecrow's head. "Go away, shoo, go on, play somewhere else." Poor Tik Tak tried to knock the crows off his head but the farmer hadn't replaced all the straw in his arms yet so he couldn't quite reach the birds. "Go away I tell you, go away." One of the crows with a grin leaned forward and pecked gently at Tik Tak's button nose. "Shoo, shoo, look the farmer is coming with his noise stick." Claw, the youngest of the crows almost fell onto the scarecrow's shoulder. "Noise stick!" he squawked, "Noise stick! You lie down and never get up if you get close to a noise stick." The crows suddenly took to the air and flapped noisily in the direction of the old windmill. "To the sails" cried Claw, "To the sails." Tik Tak shook his head and crossed his eyes to make sure that his button noise was still in place. "Yes" he whispered. "One nose, two loose pieces of straw," satisfied that everything was as it should be; he smiled and settled down once more into the early morning sun. He looked quietly in the direction of the windmill. "I hope they know," he whispered. "No place to visit, no place to stay, haunted is Dragon mill, home of the pirates." He shook his head again yawning as he did so. "I wouldn't go there, not for all the clean straw in the barn." Very soon, Tik Tak was fast asleep.

~~~

The kettle turned slowly in the middle of the stream, the early morning light reflecting off its surface as it gently bobbed to and fro. Suddenly Stitch woke a puzzled look on his face. My legs, my little legs, where are they? Shiv, Shiv, someone's stolen my legs." The little needle began to poke his friend the knife in the chest. Shiv opened one sleepy eye. "What is it this time Stitch? What's wrong?"

"Look! Look! My legs have gone. I know they were only little but I did like them really." Shiv sat up to see Stitch standing waist high in the sweet smelling meadow grass they had picked just a few hours ago. He began to smile, "You must have tucked yourself really deep down in the grass before you went to sleep, and your legs are fine." Stitch started to pull and tug at the warm grass and promptly fell onto his back, and there they were his little legs pedalling the air. "Oh hello feet, welcome back toes!" He began to clap his hands together happy to be back with his legs. Shiv in the meantime had started to climb up the grass to look over the edge of the kettle. "I can hear crow song Stitch, it must be morning," but Stitch didn't hear him, he was rolling over and over in the grass. "I've got little legs, little legs have I." The needle continued to sing and clap. Shiv noticed that the early morning mist lying close to the surface came almost up to the broken spout. He couldn't see very much at all but could hear the water. For a moment he remembered the fight of not too long ago, of Polo the Pike, Squint and Saw tooth. He almost imagined he could hear Fang's 'Tally Ho' drifting far off in the mist. "Come on Shiv, make room for me." The needle had finally got to his feet and joined his friend. "We're going the wrong way you know," said the needle suddenly. "We are floating away from the direction of our drawer in Raven Cottage."

"Don't worry, I have a plan" said Shiv. There was silence for a while as they both listened to crow song somewhere ahead in the swirling mist. "Can I see it then? Can I see this plan of yours?" Shiv turned towards the needle. "Of course not silly, it's in my head."

"Not a lot of good there is it; I can't see a plan when you're hiding it in your head?"

"Quiet! Listen!" Ahead of them could be heard a roaring noise. "Listen, it's getting louder what could it be?" The old kettle began to spin even faster as Shiv stretched as far as he could over the rim without actually falling out. "Oh no"

"What is it?" said the needle jumping up and down trying to get a better view. "It sounds like water, fast, flowing water look out Stitch, duck."

"Where, where let me see," said the little needle trying to jump even higher. "I've never seen a duck before, I've seen a toad and a pike, oh and a weasel and a cushion cat of course and."

"Get down Stitch, duck its Bracken Weir." A large dark shape appeared out of the mist. Shiv saw some weed covered wood and rusty metal bolts. The kettle raced towards the concrete blocks over which the stream waters flowed. "Ooh I'm getting dizzy Shiv, what's happening, what's happening?" Before Shiv could answer he lost his balance and fell on his head in the still warm bedding. "Get down Stitch get down," Shiv struggled to free his head from the meadow grass, with a final tug he popped free. "Down Stitch, get down". Stitch tumbled from the kettle's rim to join Shiv. "I feel dizzy Shiv, really dizzy". There was a loud noise as the kettle tipped over at an angle. "Hold on, hold on." The kettle suddenly bobbed upright only to tilt again as is was carried quickly down the weir. Suddenly it came to a halt scraping against the loose pebbly bottom of the pool. "Ooh my head," said Stitch. "I can't stand on my legs." Shiv was already making his way up and over the rim. One moment he was there, the next minute gone. Stitch started to climb after him. "Wait for me." The needle eventually reached the rim and peered over.

~~~

Down below Shiv stood ankle deep in water, balanced on a large smooth pebble. "We made it Stitch," he laughed. "We made it over Bracken Weir, come on don't be afraid jump." The little needle took a big leap landing up to his armpits in water. "Here we go all wet again. The two friends made their way carefully to the edge of the pool, slipping and sliding from one shiny pebble to another until finally they were able to clamber out and onto a dry patch of clover. Stitch began to dry himself off with the nearest leaf. "It's over Shiv, it's all over, and the bulrush can never be used again." He looked with some affection towards the old battered kettle. "Guess we are on our own now." Shiv had picked himself up; and after brushing himself down began a careful inspection of their surroundings. The early morning sun was already casting long shadows from the hedgerow that stretched away to their left. Ahead of them was an open field surrounded by a dry earthen ditch. "Hedgerow" said Shiv suddenly. "We need to get through the hedgerows and find out what lies on the other side". Stitch had finished drying himself and was listening to a sound coming from the direction of the trees. "Shiv can you hear it, it's like a funny creaking noise, listen, there it is again."

"Yes Stitch I hear it, but I don't know what it is, come on we have a lot to do." Shiv began to push his way into the hedge, deeper and deeper into the twisted branches, slowly but slowly through the cool darkness over branch and twig. "Stitch" he whispered. Are you with me?"

"Yes, yes I am." And he was.

10

HOBBLE

Hobble the Hare liked nothing more than a sunny day, he could stretch himself full length in a freshly ploughed furrow and sleep soaking up the sun, lovely sunny lazy days. Today was to be no different or so it seemed. Hobble had washed his long whiskers early at the pool, and then had a breakfast of barley shoots as he watched the early morning mist roll away from the field. He lay back as the sun climbed slowly into the morning sky. "This is the life," he whispered stretching his long brown legs. "I might hop over to see Tik Tak and Parsnip later, then again maybe I won't." He lay back perfectly still; eyes closed nothing to give away his position, save the twitch of a whisker.

~~~

"Ouch" said Stitch pulling the thorn from his elbow, "That was sharp, how much further Shiv?" The knife stopped for a moment looking back at his friend the needle. "Not far now Stitch, not very far at all."

"Don't forget though it takes me twice as long you."

"Pardon" said Shiv turning back to the branches in front of him.

"I said it takes me twice as long, you know little legs, big thorns, sore elbows and things." Shiv suddenly broke through the last branches and stepped out into the morning sun. "Hurry Stitch hurry, come and see" A long brown field stretched before him. Furrow upon furrow of freshly turned earth, somewhere ahead of him Shiv heard the creaking sound again then nothing but the breeze. Finally Stitch broke through the last bit of hedge, he was panting heavily as he reached the knife's side. "Horrible, dark and horrible - could have been anything in there. Pirates, beetles with lots of legs, weasels, and biting things like cats."

"Look, look!" said Shiv quietly, Stitch moved a little closer to his friend his words forgotten.

In the far distance the branches of a big tree danced in the wind, the mist has almost gone now the sun casting long shadows across the field. Above Shiv and Stitch the odd cloud crossed what had been a clear blue sky, and then the creaking noise again louder this time. Creak bang clatter, creak bang clatter, soft at first then louder the sound seemed to appear then disappear, one minute it was there the next it was gone. "What now" said Stitch looking up at his friend?

"Follow the furrow," said Shiv. "What can we lose yes lets follow the furrow," and they did.

~~~

Tik Tak slowly opened one eye. "No crows that's good the farmer will be pleased, he likes it when there are no crows. He may even make me a new hat, no crows oh good" he said again loudly and began to laugh. "No crows on the barley they have flown away. No crows on the barley its Tik Tak's lucky day." Suddenly he became aware of a noise behind him, "so" he whispered. "A new trick eh, creeping up on old Tik Tak, I'll show them." He flapped his arms up and down and twisted around on the stick that held him firmly to the ground. "Boo hoo higgledy doo, Tik Tak's here and he's after you." Shiv stopped suddenly shaken by the sound from the collection of rags and straw hanging from the stick. "Boo hoo higgledy doo; go away you stealers of corn, you funny looking crows, for I see no feathers!" Stitch fell over onto a pebble "Shiv what is it?"

"It's a talking turnip with a button for a nose" laughed the knife.

"How dare you my name is Tik Tak I guard the furrows so higgledy doo to you."

"Well I'm Stitch and I am a needle not a crow, I did try flying once though." Tik Tak leaned forward "You really tried flying well what happened was it fun?" The little needle looked away in embarrassment. "Didn't like it that much I fell on my head". Shiv took a step forward. "Sorry for the fright Tik Tak, we are from Raven Cottage but it's a long story."

"Told you so," said the scarecrow standing up straight again. "Ravens are part of the crow family."

"No, no" said Shiv, "Its Raven Cottage not a raven's cottage." The scarecrow thought for a moment. "Not a crow, not a raven then what?"

"Hungry" said Stitch and he was.

~~~

Sometime later after a meal of carrots Shiv and Stitch decided it was time to be on their way. They said goodbye to Tik Tak and wished him well in his fight against the crows. With a final wave they continued into the long brown furrow. It wasn't long before Stitch began to feel tired, but as far ahead of him that he could see lay only freshly turned earth.

"Hoppity up bang, bang thump, what's your game?" The large brown hare paused for breath. "Never mind what's our game, who are you?" said Shiv staring at the long eared creature that stood before him. "Hoppity up Hobble, that's what they call me."

"That's a strange name," said Stitch sitting down on top of the furrow to get his breath back. "Yes said Shiv resting for a moment. "Why do they call you Hoppity up?"

"Noise stick" replied the hare, "Farmer's noise stick, struck with a crash in my leg now it's limp, jump, limp, jump you know Hoppity up."

"Mmm sorry to hear that" said Shiv.

"Hare that, that's a good one Shiv". Stitch started to laugh; Shiv turned his attention back to the hare. "Tell me Hobble, what is the strange creaking sound we keep hearing on the wind?"

"Dragon mill" said the hare taking a quick glance back over his shoulder. "It's Dragon mill stretching its arms, dangerous place, worse than noise sticks, no one treads the stubble at Dragon mill many have tried and many have failed Hoppity up, bang, bang thump, suns high, must rest now."

"Mmm" said Stitch rubbing his sore elbow.

"Nice to have met you then Hobble" said the knife preparing to leave. "Just one thing, if you don't mind." Again the hare took a quick look over his shoulder. "Why dangerous?"

"Oh! Didn't I tell you" said Hobble preparing to leave. "The Pike wood Pirates, yes the home of the Pike wood Pirates. Farewell Shiv and Stitch of the little legs."

With a single jump and limp, Hobble disappeared into the field. "Did you hear that Shiv, he said I've got little legs?"

"Well you have haven't you" said Shiv starting to smile. Stitch rubbed his elbow again. The knife and the needle continued their journey following the furrow in the direction of Dragon mill.

~~~

Ragweed the rat puffed and panted as he dragged the heavy piece of sacking up the last two wooden steps that lead to the big round millwheel. "There we go" he said dropping the sack on the smooth stone, "come on Wrinkle hurry up with that other sacking." His friend sneezed as he continued to drag the old flour sack across the dusty floor, Ragweed hopped up onto a wooden shelf careful not catch his feet in a rusty old mousetrap by a broken pickle jar. He reached forward and wiped the tiny pane of glass with his paw then; balancing carefully on one leg he put his nose up against the window and looked out.

"Oh to be a pirate a pirate I would be, what do you say Wrinkle?"

"I'd say all this dust is getting up my nose a pirate on the sea, all I want to do, is sneeze Achoo."

"Aye, aye Wrinkle, if its pirates we are to be, then pirates we shall be." Their laughter hung in the air and very soon it was gone.

~~~

"Look, look" cried Stitch. "It's the mill, the waving arms of Dragon mill." Shiv stood for a moment looking at the old windmill, its big sails broken. He saw, holes in the roof, and white paint long since faded making way for climbing ivy and willow. Dragon mill's tiller lay almost buried beneath a blackberry bush. But it was Stitch who found the old doorway now covered by planks and rusty nails. "It doesn't look very frightening does it Shiv?"

"Something is just not right here," said the knife, "it's too quiet" And it was.

11

DRAGON MILL

Ragweed removed a piece of a blackbird's eggshell from his tooth. "Mmm, tasty any more in there Wrinkle?" The large brown rat popped his head up over the edge of the nest high up beneath the long since silent mill. From where he stood Wrinkle could see Ragweed balanced carefully on a beam down below. "Sorry that's all Raggy there's no more eggs just feathers and things."

"Don't call me Raggy, its Ragweed to you, now hurry back down here there's work to do and plenty of it." Ragweed kicked the remains of the little s blue off the beam and then dropping onto all fours began to run towards the windmills cracked window.

~~~

"Ouch, ouch" cried Stitch. "Stinging sticks Shiv help me, help me these sticks are stinging my legs." Shiv reached down and lifted Stitch clear of the nettle patch that he had stepped into. "Thanks Shiv I'm sore all over it's even worse than having little legs this is." Shiv placed the needle onto a piece of ground close to the ivy that covered the brickwork of the deserted mill. "Mmm" said Shiv suddenly "how do we get in, this door is sealed?"

"Get in, what do you mean get in, I'm not going in there for anything or anybody, you heard what Tik Tak and Hobble said about climbing. I don't like it Shiv, its dark, and they said it is very, very dangerous. I know, why don't you climb up while I wait here and keep guard you know on the lookout for pirates, and weasels and things?"

"Stinging sticks" said Shiv suddenly. "Stinging sticks, and very soon darkness will be with us, come on onto my shoulders you'll be okay." Stitch climbed slowly onto his friend's shoulders and began to hold on tightly to Shiv's neck. "Not so tight Stitch, I can't breathe." Shiv began the long journey up the ivy upwards towards a small faraway window. "Hold on Stitch, this won't take long."

~~~

Ragweed stepped out of the shadows and moved on tiptoe up the old rickety steps of the mill, past the mill wheel, climbing until he reached the shelf just below the window. "Up you come "he whispered "come and shake hands with the Pike wood Pirates, very, very soon

48

you'll be visitors in our cellar of doom." He waved with his sharp claws for Wrinkle to join him.

Upwards, upwards Shiv paused for breath trying to work out how much further the cracked and broken window was, "hey Stitch."

"What" said the little needle, eyes shut tight.

"I can see twisted tree from here, and he could.

~~~

All was not well in the wood many of the creatures living there were afraid of the rats that had taken over the old mill. The rats had stolen eggs and destroyed nests. The carts used by the squirrels for carrying the nuts collected for the long winter that lay ahead had been overturned. Worst though was in store for Blink the river vole, when after a struggle his boat had been sunk. Now the elders gathered beneath the roots of Burnt Oak. The huge cavern once the home of very old badgers had become a place of safety in dangerous times. "Who's going to remove the rats then, and who is going to volunteer to get them out of Dragon mill?" The dormouse spoke a little louder.

"Come now there must be someone brave enough do you hear me I want my acorns back." Lots of bright eyes stared back at him from the darkness but the great cavern of Burnt Oak remained silent.

~~~

Shiv pulled himself carefully up onto the wooden frame of the window and looked inside. "Seems very quiet Stitch, empty and quiet, I think I can just about get through this gap, come on Stitch climb down and I'll help you through." The little needle climbed down from his friends back not daring to look at where they had just come from. "Come on Stitch careful now." Shiv and Stitch tugged and pushed, pushed and tugged, until finally they stood on the dust-covered shelf inside the mill. "How do we get down Shiv and what do we do when we reach the ground?" The needle looked around he suddenly felt dizzy as he spotted the dusty wooden floor far below. "We find somewhere warm to rest," said the knife, "at least it's nice and dry in here." Stitch took a step forward,

"Shiv you are sure you have never been here before?

"No you know I haven't."

49

"And it is empty and old and not lived in like you said isn't it?"

"Of course it's not lived in."

"Oh dear then whose are those footprints on that beam over there?"

"Ah, ah welcome to Dragon mill pointy." A large frightening looking rat stepped from behind a half empty pickle jar just to Shiv's left. "Pirates Shiv Pike wood Pirates, run, run." Ragweed made his way slowly towards Shiv and Stitch his sharp claws moving left and right, right and left just in front of them. "Jump, jump" cried Shiv, "look there's sacking below, jump Stitch jump," with a hop and a skip the knife disappeared over the edge of the shelf. "Oh help, help" cried Stitch running as fast as his little legs would carry him; he jumped into the air just as Ragweed's claws dug into the beam where he had been standing. The little needle fell head over heels, and landed with a thump in a cloud of dust on top of one of the old flour sacks left there earlier by Ragweed and Wrinkle.

High up inside the roof Ragweed began to run along the beams and was soon joined by Wrinkle, together they made their way quickly towards the ground below where they could see Shiv and Stitch beginning to get back on their feet. The knife and the needle brushed themselves down quickly looking around for somewhere safe to hide. Stitch coughed and began to limp towards an upturned box near the millstone. "No Stitch they will soon get into that, if you can they can," Stitch began to mumble.

"Safe he said, quiet he said didn't say anything about being eaten by a hungry rat."

"Save your breath Stitch," said the knife joining him. "It won't be long before they reach us we must hide."

~~~

Suddenly there was a loud scream from somewhere above them. Shiv looked up quickly to see Wrinkly flying through the air tail held in the mouth of a very big owl. "Romulus" said Shiv and Stitch together; this is the home of Romulus of the Rafters.

The great owl flew higher and higher until it became almost invisible in the shadows at the top of the mill, for a moment there was silence and then. "Wrinkle" screamed Ragweed come on Wrinkly, where are you?" Nothing but silence and dust then a noise and Wrinkle suddenly appeared from behind a beam. "Ouch ooh, he bit my tail, he did you know, and I banged my head on a rafter, look at this lump its ever so big, and look, look at my tail it's all bent now." He stopped to rub the lump on his head.

"How did you get away?" said Ragweed patting his friend on the back.

"I bit his leg and he dropped me, I landed on my head, it didn't half hurt."

"Come on Wrinkle we need time to rest and plan, the pointy ones are going nowhere, and we will soon make them pay."

"Well my head still hurts," said Wrinkle. "Are you going to bandage my tail"? The rats stepped into the shadows and disappeared.

~~~

"That was close," said Shiv looking for somewhere to sit down. "I told you things would work out okay."

"I know it was close," said the needle. "Too close, I want to go home, I'm fed up I want my drawer back, I've had enough of stoats and weasels, beetles and fish, I'm tired, I'm sore, my elbow hurts, my ears are full of flour dust, I'm hungry and, and"

"Yes," said the knife starting to smile.

"Stitch started to laugh. "And yes, I've only got little legs."

12

ESCAPE

It was sometime before Shiv and Stitch reached the safety of the mills rusty old gears and now they sat quietly trying to decide what to do next. "If we leave the mill Shiv where will we go, there are rats in here and rats out there, what will we do?" Shiv thought for a moment. "There may be a way, remember when we reached the window and I said I could see Twisted Tree?"

"Yes," said the little needle shuddering at the thought.

"Well I saw something else from up there."

"Yes I bet you did, how far down it was to fall."

"No, no listen it was a possible way back to Raven Cottage, yes a way back home." Stitch banged his head on one of the gears in excitement. "Ouch, way home, ooh that hurt, a way back to our friends in the kitchen?"

"Maybe Stitch just maybe."

"Come on tell me please how do we do it, how do we escape the weasels and the rats?"

"We walk the wires Stitch, we just walk the wires."

~~~

It had taken Ragweed a really long time to move out from the shadows and onto the beam; he moved slowly very slowly getting nearer and nearer until he was just a few feet above the knife and needle's hiding place in the machinery. "So" he whispered, "walking the wires eh, we will see about that, I think you are about to get a surprise and one you won't like my little pointed friends," a chuckle escaped before he could stop it.

"What was that?" said Stitch banging his head again. "Ouch my head will soon be the same size as my legs."

"Quiet Stitch quiet, it seems to be coming from the beam above us but at least it's safe here." Stitch was busy rubbing the little bump that had appeared on his head. "What's a walking wire Shiv, does it bite or sting?"

"No my friend there will be no more stinging or biting."

Ragweed sniggered again from his hiding place above them. "That's what you think pointy; it will sting alright, oh yes indeed," he slipped quietly back into the shadows. "Time to contact the Pike wood Pirates, soon we will welcome Captain No-bones back to Dragon mill."

~~~

Deep underground beneath the roots of Burnt Oak, the meeting of the elders had come to a noisy end. The dormouse was still unhappy about his acorns but at least the others had decided to try and get help. Rosehip who had been visiting a relative in Pike wood had joined the meeting and had mentioned the strange appearance of shiny points on the lawn at Raven Cottage. "Maybe they could help," suggested the timid little dormouse. "Maybe they have other shiny point friends."

"Here, here" came a voice out of the darkness, "and who then will seek out the pointy ones". All eyes turned to rest upon the dormouse.

"Well I do want my acorns back, very well then I'll go and see twelve trees of the stream perhaps he will know how we might contact them."

"Then it is decided," said the badger limping forward for he was very old now and unable to leave the safety of Burnt Oak. "Go then with courage little one and bring back news of these visitors to our wood." There was a sound of scurrying in the darkness and very soon the chamber was empty.

~~~

"It's very, very quiet Shiv, do you think it's safe to leave now?"

"We have no choice Stitch, we must do something before Ragweed and Wrinkle return or worse still call their friends."

"I'm frightened," said the needle.

"You're not the only one Stitch so am I, come on let's go we have to find a way back up onto the sails."

"Up" said the needle shaking his head, "up, but we've only just come down."

"I'm sorry Stitch but it's the only way."

They crept carefully on tiptoe and peered around the edge of the rusting machinery. "What do you think Stitch" whispered the knife. "Up the staircase" the little needle thought for a moment. "If the rats return they will see us," Shiv looked down at his friend.

"I can't climb again so soon Stitch my arms still ache, come on its now or never." They ran quickly but quietly to the foot of the old stone staircase. "Are you ready Stitch"?

"I'm ready," Shiv was the first to reach up onto the cold stone step.

"Here we go again," he whispered to his friend then glancing round stepped forward.

The climb seemed to take forever, stopping and starting to make sure they were not being followed, but eventually they finally reached the top and paused for breath. Shiv was looking carefully at the long wooden beam that ran the full width of the mill. "That's the way out onto the sails Stitch, we have to squeeze through that gap over there, now can you see where that beam of light is hitting the floor?"

"Yes Shiv I see it but."

"No but's Stitch trust me have I ever let you down?"

"Well" began the needle, "can you remember when we."

"Never mind" said Shiv starting to pull himself up onto the beam "never mind", he started to crawl along the wood towards the light in no time at all Stitch joined him and they continued their journey in silence.

~~~

The dormouse stepped back into the shadows on the edge of Pike wood and stood nibbling on an acorn. "Mmm this is good tender and juicy." The acorn gradually began to disappear towards the cup, "Ah that's better perhaps a little snooze before I continue my journey in search of the shiny points. He slid very slowly down into the soft moss that grew at the base of the tree and very soon was fast asleep.

~~~

Shiv was first to emerge from the hole and onto the beam. He waited quietly for his friend Stitch and as he did so he began to pace up and down and then suddenly he began to jump. Stitch emerged from the mill to see Shiv running up and down on the crippled sail. "Shiv, Shiv what are you doing?"

"Ssshh, hop, skip three four, hop skip twice more." Stitch sat down on the beam puzzled by his friend's strange behaviour. "He looks like twelve trees in a hurry" he thought to himself. "Hop skip three four, hop skip twice more, that's it that's it, Stitch listen this is what we do."

"No shouldn't it be hop skip, hop skip nine ten eleven twelve bit more something hum de ho?"

"Stitch what are you talking about?"

"Little legs Shiv I need more steps."

"Little legs" Shiv laughed.

~~~

Far below at the edge of the blackberry thicket a small band of rats had slipped out of the shadows and stood silently looking upwards in the direction of Ragweed's claws. "There they are boss," a large brown rat pushed Ragweed roughly to one side unclipping a small telescope from his belt as he did so the evil looking rat steadied the lens over his lieutenant's back and began to focus on Shiv and Stitch far above on the mill. Hiccup and trig were new to the pirate band and stood quietly at the back watching their new boss.

"Why do they call him No-Bones Trig?"

"Because he's famous and a hero, did you know he can squeeze through any gap no matter how small, he once escaped from a jumping jaw." Hiccup took a deep breath.

"No I don't believe it nobody escapes the jaw, it snaps down and crushes all your bones and then that's it you're done for," a small shudder ran through Trigs tail.

"They say it broke every bone in his body and now he can pass through the smallest place." Hiccup turned back to look at No-Bones. "Rubbish, somebody else told me he fell off a wall."

"Well why did you ask then?" said Trig losing interest.

No-Bones carefully replaced the telescope in his belt and turned back to the other pirates. "Ragweed you've done well today."

"What about me sir" said Wrinkle easily identified by the bandage on his tail.

"Aye you too, now how do we get into the mill?"

"Follow Me," whispered Ragweed feeling important. *In no time at all they had entered Dragon mill and began to make their way up the staircase towards the upper chamber.*

~~~

"What now Shiv I've practiced and practiced until I nearly fell off."

That's the general idea Stitch."

"What is?"

"Falling off,"

"Falling off" Stitch stood mouth wide open. "Falling off are you mad?"

"No but they are," Shiv pointed down below just as the last few rats disappeared into the ivy.

"Are we in trouble again Shiv are we?"

"We are."

<u>13</u>

PERIL IN PIKE WOOD

The dormouse stretched his arms and yawned. "Sleep" he mumbled, "lovely warm sleep no rats, no shiny points, oh dear oh dear" he said quickly getting to his feet. "Shiny points I had almost forgotten all about them, I must find them before darkness falls." He brushed himself down and with a last yawn slowly made his way towards the hedgerow. "Why me" he thought, "I'm really small I am, I bet nobody is as small as me." But he was wrong wasn't he.

~~~

Stitch started to crawl back along the beam towards the hole. "Falling off, no way I will not fall off, jump or be pushed from all the way up here by you or anybody else; I am not falling off no."

"But you'll be ripped to pieces if those rats catch up with you," said the knife turning his back on his friend. Stitch stopped and looked back. "Rats oh yes the rats I'd forgotten about them. What now then, I suppose its run, hop skippety drop?"

"Not quite Stitch, not quite, Look over there past the sail, do you see it?"

"See what" said the needle leaning forward as far as he could. "There's only an old horse trough filled with water."

"That's right Stitch."

"You don't mean, you can't mean, no, not jump off the sails into that?"

"Your choice Stitch, it's either that or the rats." Suddenly a huge brown face full of teeth pushed its way through the gap just where the needle was sitting. "Come on" screamed No-Bones, "we'll have them in seconds." The rat cleared the gap and began to move slowly towards Shiv and Stitch. "No turning back now come on lads there's a meal waiting."

Shiv and Stitch took one look at each other and started to run down the beam of the old sail, "come on." Three rats had now appeared from inside Dragon mill and carefully digging their claws into the rotten wood began to move forward.

"Remember what I said Stitch hop, skip, three, four, hop skip once more". They sailed out into space and began to fall. Shiv and Stitch landed in the trough with a mighty splash.

"Ooh its cold and it's gone up my nose Shiv." The knife was already beginning to clamber up the stone sides and out of the freezing water. "Come on Stitch reach up, I'll pull you clear." He leaned forward and lifted the little needle high into the air clear of the water. "There Stitch you'll soon dry off."

"Look" said Stitch pointing up at the sails. Shiv finally pulled himself out of the water and gazed upwards, they both watched as little brown grey shapes ran up and down to and fro. High above Shiv and Stitch, No-Bones wasn't very happy.

"What do you mean they've jumped, how could they have jumped it's too high?" His claws continued to dig into the wooden sail. "Fell in the horse trough boss, I can see them, wet through they are."

"You'll be wet through in a minute, I'll have you walking the sail and you can join them." Ragweed took a step back. "Not my fault boss honest, Pointy stood on my foot and then made a run for it." No-Bones edged a little closer to the sails edge. "Soon my pointed friends, yes very soon you will be mine, right you lot into the mill with you. Come on, come on we need a plan."

"Aye, aye boss, aye, aye."

~~~

Down below Shiv and Stitch had jumped down onto the dry dusty soil and with a last glance upwards saw the rats disappearing back into the mill. "They won't give up Shiv, they will be even angrier now, all that anger with teeth." Shiv continued to wring the water out of his jacket. "We need a hiding place and quick," said Shiv. "Before the rats reach us."

"It's not fair I can't run quickly I can't jump far, I must have the littlest legs in the whole world."

You're wrong my friend, I have." the dormouse stepped out from behind a fresh molehill.

"come on, quickly now," said the little mouse. "I've been sent by my friends from the chamber of Burnt Oak to find you we need your help."

"You need our help?" said Shiv moving towards the tiny mouse, "seems to me we need yours."

"Can you run very, very fast?" said the dormouse suddenly.

"I can't but I feel really sorry for you because your legs are smaller than mine."

"Ah yes true," said the dormouse smiling. "But the difference here you see is that I have four, come along now hurry, hurry." The mouse ran quickly back into the ditch by the hedgerow, "Follow me, "Shiv and Stitch and the strange little creature began to run, down the ditch that led back to pike wood, jumping cracks, fallen branches and stones until suddenly the mouse stopped. "It's too late look, look on the edge of the wood," all three of them looked carefully over the ditch. "Rats" said the mouse.

"Lots of them" said Shiv. Stitch sat down and crossed his arms.

"Rats plus more rats, plus a few more rats that means big sharp hungry trouble."

~ ~ ~

"Spread out" whispered No-Bones removing a very sharp thorn from his belt. "Ragweed, you and Wrinkle take the left, you two over to that burrow on the right, the rest of you follow me". No-Bones waved the thorn in the air. "Come on boys there's only one place they can be."

"The ditch" was the single cry.

"Yes lads the ditch, now there can be no escape, keep your eyes peeled." Shiv and Stitch watched as the fearsome looking rats got closer and closer. "Now what Shiv, there's nowhere to run". The rats were getting nearer and nearer, Stitch could now see row upon row of sharp shiny teeth. "Shiv, Shiv what are we going to do?" Suddenly the dormouse was knocked off his feet as the ground before them exploded. Soil flew everywhere and then suddenly from the centre of the mound a black soil covered nose appeared. "Hello, just in time it seems," it was Short tail.

"Hurray, hurray hello again," Stitch stood up clapping his hands.

"Quickly no time to waste into my tunnel I can get you safely past the pirates." Shiv dived head first into the tunnel crawling out of sight on hands and knees, the mouse soon followed. "Bit dark isn't it," said Stitch, "bit dark in there?"

"What's it to be Stitch my dark tunnel or a rat's dark stomach?"

"Coming," said the needle. He ran up the slope and disappeared down into the darkness. Short tail took one last quick look around to get his bearings and then backed into the tunnel sealing it behind him. "Shiv where are you, ouch what's that."

"That's my elbow," said the knife "careful now just follow the sounds in front."

59

"I bet there are worms in here lots of them and horrible slimy things." A little voice ahead of him floated back "that's my breakfast, dinner and supper you're talking about. "In no time at all Shiv, Stitch, Short tail and the mouse emerged from the tunnel close to the trees. Behind them they could hear No-Bones screaming with anger at losing them. "Thanks Short tail you really saved the day."

The mole blushed "what are friends for?"

"Well not for sharing worms," said Stitch brushing the soil from his jacket.

"Goodbye then and good luck," Short tail disappeared beneath a fresh mound of soil.

"Come now," said the mouse "it's not far." Soon they could see the twisted roots of Burnt Oak before them. "At last" cried the mouse I'm finally home. After a rest and refreshment Shiv and Stitch were invited to tell their story to the elders as the woodland creatures gathered in the cavern. The badger listened patiently to their tale. "So shiny points if you can reach Raven Cottage do you think your friends would join you to defeat the Pike wood Pirates?"

"But of course" said the knife.

"Let it be then."

"You mean you can get us to Raven Cottage?"

"Of course" smiled the badger.

"Home Shiv", Stitch jumped up and down. "At last we're going home, yes going home."

14

NO-BONES

"Quickly everybody quickly, there are rats in the tunnels, its No-Bones and the Pirates. Move the young ones out of the nursery, what are we to do?" The grey squirrel that had arrived with this news dropped to his knees, paws over his eyes. "I led them here, they followed me, I'm sure they did oh I'm so sorry."

"More trouble" said the needle.

"More trouble" said the knife. The sound of snapping teeth seemed to get closer and closer as echoes bounced down the long entrance to the main chamber. Another squirrel limped into the chamber short of breath and holding his elbow. "Some evil rat called Rag tooth bit my arm, I brushed my tail up his nose and made him sneeze, and they don't like the dark tunnel too much these rats. About a dozen of them are inching their way slowly towards us. We need a plan and we need it now." Thoughts of fear and danger spread quickly among all the animals as they set about preparing for the worse. All the young one's from the nursery were walking on tip toe or were being carried silently to one of the storage tunnels. Several of the mice, distant cousins to the rats, were arming themselves with small round pebbles, building a pile next to the twisted roots that struggled out of the wall. Suddenly a rather frightened looking rabbit hopped out of the tunnel. "They want the shiny points it's not us they're after." Shiv and Stitch looked at each other.

"Short tail we need your help, over here we have a plan." At that moment a fierce looking rat burst into the chamber. "Come on boys, I have them." The rat leapt forward snatching Stitch up in his jaws and with a cry of victory turned back in the direction he had come from. The blow across No-Bones' back was powerful and painful. He let out a cry dropping Stitch roughly to the floor. "hey you bony," shouted Stitch picking himself up and running back to where his friend stood." Has anybody ever told you that you you've got bad breath, oh and by the way I would get those teeth seen too it looks like you need a filling." Another tremendous blow caught the rat across the shoulders as he turned half stumbling only to come face to face with the badger. "So old Brock, woke you up did I, you won't be so lucky next time." The sharp claws of his right leg flashed out leaving a deep mark in the fur on the badger's side. The badger reared up springing forward and bit No-Bones very firmly on the nose. The rat sat back, tears now running from his eyes. "You bit me, I can't believe it you bit my nose, you can't bite my nose what will the others think now it's not right you know."

"No it's your nose" shouted Stitch laughing. The old badger growled and took a step forward. "Be gone from here you evil creature." The rat still clutching his throbbing nose scampered back towards the tunnel just as Ragweed and Wrinkle emerged looking for a fight. "Captain, captain your nose it's all well sort of bent and twisted and sort of a reddish colour," the rat couldn't speak any more for laughing. Ragweed stepped forward, "want a bandage boss?" No-Bones kicked him hard.

"I'll give you bandage, you'll be wearing one in a minute. Back to the mill, we need to come up with a new plan."

"What sort of plan boss one where you don't get bitten on the nose?"

"Very funny well we could start by making you go first instead of me who knows he might attack you." Ragweed started to laugh.

"And what's so funny?" the rat started to laugh louder now.

"Who knows get it boss, a joke?" He didn't.

~ ~ ~

"Collapse the tunnel you say?" Short tail adjusted his glasses. "Sounds good but I can't do it alone, I'll need help."

"You dig, Stitch me and the others will shovel, everyone can help."

"But what about the rats" said a little dormouse hiding behind the bushy tail of a squirrel?

"They must be at the entrance to the tunnel" said Shiv, "where it slopes up into daylight. We can start digging around the first bend. With lots of help we can have it blocked before they find out what's happening. Come on everybody but quickly we don't want them to find out about our plans too soon."

The little band of woodland creatures led by Short tail, Shiv and Stitch crept slowly down into the darkness careful to listen for the return of the rats. Suddenly Shiv brought everyone to a halt. "Listen! Listen!" The voice of No-Bones drifted in from darkness. "It's up to you now Ragweed I'm off to get help from cousin One Eye, I hear he's over at Twisted Tree. It shouldn't take too long remember I want the shiny point back in Dragon mill by teatime." the whispers died away and silence returned to the tunnel. "It's now or never short tail" said Shiv. "Dig my friend dig for all your worth," and he did. For the next few minutes everyone worked in silence shoving and pushing, pushing and shoving, lifting and shifting, shifting and lifting and very soon the tunnel began to fill with damp dark soil.

~~~

At the entrance to Burnt Oak Ragweed had gathered the rats around him, "Fire" he said suddenly. "Fire what catapults, cannons, what?" said Wrinkle.

"No stupid, fire lovely glowing hot fire."

"You don't mean."

"Yes" said Ragweed, "smoke them out."

"Oh" said Wrinkle looking disappointed, "I thought we were going to set fire to them." Ragweed hit him with a bandage "Come on, No-Bones will be returning soon, gather twigs and branches." The evil looking rats set about their task.

~~~

"What now" said Stitch trying to remove soil from his ears with a finger, Short tail suddenly stepped forward "What I can fill in, I can also open up." He explained that while Shiv and Stitch continued their journey to Raven Cottage he would build a new entrance on the far side of the old tree, one to be known only to the animals. Everyone clapped and laughed with happiness as the mole disappeared into the darkness.

~~~

Outside the rats lit the fire and waited, as white smoke drifted into the tunnel only to blow back in their faces. "It's blocked Raggy, they've blocked the tunnel."

Raggy coughed and took a step back "Oh no, No-Bones won't like this." The rats turned silently and heads hung low made their way slowly across the furrowed field towards Dragon mill.

15

RETURN TO RAVENS

"It's a tunnel" said Shiv looking at the large hole in front of him.

"Oh no not another tunnel Shiv, I'm still finding soil everywhere, look here's a bit in my shoe," he lifted his foot up to show the knife and fell over. All the creatures gathered around him, laughed and reached forward to help him up, the elderly badger shuffled forward. "It is called a warren and is the home of many rabbits, one of the tunnels passes under the stream and ends near the house of glass. Shiv and Stitch looked at each other,

"Rosehip, said Shiv"

"Yes and Briar and Nettle said Stitch, so that's how they managed to disappear so quickly." The badger waited a moment before he spoke again. "We can take you as far as the house of glass unseen and unheard by anyone other than our own kind."

"Cushion Cat" said Stitch suddenly; the badger looked on, a puzzled expression on his face.

"I know of many woodland folk, but I've never heard of a Cushion Cat."

"It's nothing" said Shiv, "please continue."

"Yes, yes," said the badger, "you can return to pike wood in the same way unseen then you and the other shiny points and ourselves can attack." Shiv and Stitch thanked the badger and said goodbye to the dormouse and his friends and then stepped into the burrow. Stitch stopped for a moment and turned back he quickly ran across to where the dormouse was standing. "Goodbye my friend, we'll see you soon, oh and by the way I like the little legs." The burrow was light with lots of room, Shiv noticed roots hanging from the roof and he noticed something else too, as they made their way further into the tunnel they seemed to be walking downhill. "Stitch, Stitch have you noticed that the tunnel is dropping away from us?"

"Yes" said the needle, "I'm almost running."

"Stop, what's that?" Stitch almost bumped into his friend.

"No it can't be, it sounds like, no not here?" They rounded a bend in the tunnel.

"It is" said Stitch, dark dirty muddy water had broken through and had been filling the tunnel and now blocked their way. It's not fair" said Stitch, "we've come all this way so close to home now we are going to have to go all that way back again. " He began to beat his hands against the wall and stamp his feet on the muddy soil. "Not fair, not fair."

One Eye the sly jumped from his hiding place in the watery tunnel and sank his teeth into the material of Stitch's shirt. "Now I have you pointy," before the knife could speak the rat ran into the water and then with a sudden splash was gone. Shiv fell down onto his knees. "Stitch, oh no Stitch after all this time," not even a bubble broke the surface of the water. "I have to find a way to rescue Stitch he's my best friend what will I do?"

"Very little" said the evil rat as it reappeared from the water moving towards Shiv, water dripping from the wet fur on his back. "But I thought," said Shiv and he pressed himself closer to the tunnel wall. "You thought the entire tunnel was full of water didn't you, well it's not it's only a few feet deep."

"Where's Stitch, where's my friend?"

"Oh he's hanging around," said One Eye reaching for Shiv, "just hanging around." He returned quickly to the water with Shiv firmly clenched in his jaws and disappeared beneath the surface. Stitch was still coughing as One Eye resurfaced from the water with Shiv. He threw the knife out the darkness up onto dry dusty soil and stepped ashore himself. "So pointy you are my prisoner at last. Remember my boat and how you destroyed it, you hadn't reckoned on my cousin had you?" He picked Shiv up quickly and turned in the direction of the needle. "Hear that Stitch" said Shiv still struggling to escape, "One eye has a cousin."

"Some relative" said the needle starting to dry off, who would want to be his cousin?"

"Why, cousin No-Bones of course, king of the mill" said the rat, Shiv let out a deep sigh. One Eye the sly stood back grinning at Shiv and Stitch as they struggled helplessly both now held securely by the tree's roots. "It's been a long time pointy, but now my revenge is complete. Why don't you hang around a little longer while I go and tell Squint and Saw tooth, I'm sure they will be pleased to see you?" He began to laugh, "now then don't go away will you." The laughter echoed around the tunnel and then suddenly he was gone. "Twisted Tree" said Stitch struggling on the broken root, "its Twisted Tree Shiv, I recognise that place over there, remember when I fell down that hole, yes its Twisted Tree all right." Shiv turned to look at his friend and as he did so the root he was hanging on began to move. "I don't know about Twisted Tree Stitch but he's definitely twisted and evil and he means to do us no good." The root snapped Shiv fell heavily rolled over and came to rest up against the tunnel wall; he quickly got to his feet and limped over to the way out. "Wait for me Shiv please."

"Ssshh" said the knife "quiet now I must check the way is clear", he looked into the darkness listening for the sound of any movement, but there was nothing just the sound of his own breathing. The knife began to shiver he was cold and wet but at least I'm free he thought to himself. "Come on Shiv please help me down." Shiv made his way back to the main tunnel and after a struggle and a tug the needle stood before him. The journey down the remaining part of tunnel had been quite frightening, at any moment Shiv and Stitch expected to see One Eye the sly returning with Squint and Saw tooth. Soon they began the long climb back up to the surface Shiv of course reached the surface first and popped his head out for a quick look, he could see the sun slowly beginning to set in the sky and strawberries, he could smell strawberries. In no time at all Stitch joined him and together they began the final part of their journey. "Look" cried the needle "Kipper's Kingdom, I wonder if Compo is still making a mess of his web."

"And what about Monty" said Shiv, they travelled onwards past the barn and very soon reached the border of the lawn. The smell of strawberries was even stronger now carried by the cool evening breeze. "Look, look" cried Stitch with excitement "it's the plant pot we can't be far away now." They pushed into the long waving grass.

"Hey," Stitch fell head over heels.

"Oh sorry" said the needle getting to his feet "it's the house carrier Shiv; there must be a few around here."

"A few, a few, no I'm the only one you nearly fell over me last time you was here." Shiv and Stitch looked at each other then looked back at the snail. "Well they are heavy you know, you can't run everywhere."

"I know what you mean," said the needle "I've only got little legs."

"You're lucky," said the snail slowly.

"Lucky, you think I'm lucky to have little legs why do you say that?"

"Well I suppose it's because I haven't got any," said the snail popping back into his shell Stitch stepped forward and knocked loudly. "I don't believe you, how can you not have any legs?"

"Look" said Shiv with a whisper.

"What is it Shiv did you hear what the house carrier just said I don't believe it but he said he doesn't have any legs, not even little ones do you think it's true?"

"Forget the snail Stitch; forget about the rats and everything else because here is the best sight of all. The one we have been waiting for." Raven Cottage stood bathed in the golden light of a setting sun. "I can't believe it," said Stitch gazing at the cottage in the distance, "home our very own home at last; I can't wait to tell Percy and the others about our adventures. Shiv stood quietly hands in pockets, looking back at Twisted Tree.

"You know Stitch my friend that was close very close, we almost didn't make it."

"No" said the needle. "But here we are and before long we can join our friends in the drawer."

"I think perhaps you are forgetting something Stitch."

"No, no I think I've got everything."

"The cushion cat, what about the cushion cat?" Stitch continued to look at the cottage.

"Well I have had to fight rats, weasels, more rats, stoats, big rats, I've nearly drowned and I've fell over a snail, oh and I fell on my head when I tried to fly, so I'm not bothered about a big bundle of fur."

"Look," said the knife "over there do you see it?" A huge orange shape was moving along the hedgerow towards the cottage. "It's the cushion cat isn't it Shiv?"

"I'm afraid it is Stitch, do you feel like a bit of climbing?" They left the lawn and stepped into the flowers near the rusty fence. "I suppose we are going to have to go back in the way we came out," whispered the needle feeling a little afraid."

"Cock a doodle how do you do."

"What was that," Stitch stumbled and fell over again.

"I said cock a doodle, doodle how do you do," Shiv took a step forward.

"Hello I don't believe we have met before,"

"My name is Sage the cockerel." By now Stitch had managed to get back onto his feet again. "Hey you I'm a very curious Cockerel, you don't have any any cousins called One Eye or No-Bones?"

"No, no" said the bird strutting forward ruffling his feathers, "but I do have a brother called Peck," Stitch almost laughed, Shiv took yet another step forward.

"Have you seen a cat?" he whispered.

"Oh cock a doodle twizzle, the great big orange cat with gleaming teeth, bright eyes and a slight limp?"

"Yes, yes that's the one."

"No, sorry I haven't," with that the bird pecked at the ground and headed off down the garden. Shiv and Stitch watched the cockerel disappear into the distance.

"I wonder if he knows about Fang," whispered Stitch to himself.

"What was that Stitch?"

"Nothing," "listen can you hear that?"

"Not again" said the knife "what is it this time."

"Me that's what," Shiv couldn't believe what he saw.

"But you're supposed to be."

"Yes supposed to be at Dragon mill, well I'm not am I?" Captain No-Bones leader of the Pike wood Pirates and cousin to One Eye the Sly stood before them, "It's time for revenge."

"I reckon I'm off," said the needle, quickly dashing into the rose garden and was soon joined by Shiv. "There is no escape from me and my lads."

"This isn't happening," said the needle, "I'm only a few feet away from safety and my warm drawer."

"Our drawer", corrected Shiv.

"And here we go again, one mean looking, I'll never give up chasing you, rat is all that stands between us and freedom.

"Not quite Stitch."

"What do you mean?"

"Look" two more evil looking rats had joined No-Bones, "more trouble Stitch."

"Shiv, cats do they like cockerels and rats and things?"

"Why?"

"Well unless I am mistaken the cushion cat has reached the gate."

"Captain be careful sir, there's a furry fangs, a big furry fangs coming up behind us."

"So" said the evil looking rat, looking towards the rose bushes. "This time they win again, but one day my cousin and I."

"Was that One Eye or two?" said Stitch.

"Laugh you may little one, but Captain No-Bones has the making of you and I'll be back that's a promise."

"Well boo hoo, higgledy doo" said the needle; the rat took a step forward.

"You'll feel my claws and teeth one day, one day and soon," he turned to leave. "Come then boys back to Dragon mill." By the time Twizzle arrived in front of the cottage the rats had gone, the cat lazily sniffed the air, took a quick look round and slipped through the flap in the door.

~ ~ ~

For a while Shiv and Stitch sat back enjoying the setting sun, taking in the smells and the sounds of the garden, happy for a few moments to rest and think about all that had happened.

"Shiv"

"Yes," said the knife beginning to get to his feet ready for the final part of their journey.

"Why don't snails have legs, and if it's true that they really don't have legs how do they move?"

"Slowly" said Shiv smiling "very slowly." In no time at all the knife and the needle reached to cat flap cut into the cottage door, "Well Stitch almost home." Shiv stepped forward gently pushing the flap as he did so.

"I wouldn't, no I wouldn't really do that."

"What was that", the flap swung back almost knocking Shiv over.

"It was me and I wouldn't do that," a small robin hopped down from the hedge and landed quietly on a milk bottle. "Big monster in there full of teeth, loves feathers and beaks."

"Well thank you for the warning my friend but we don't have feathers and beaks."

"Okay, but don't say I didn't warn you," The robin flew back to the safety of its nest in the hedge. Once again Shiv pushed the flap forward and looked inside. "All clear Stitch, come on hurry."

"Are you sure, are you really sure?"

"Of course I am" said the knife, and with that he disappeared inside, Stitch took one last look behind him and quickly followed his friend into the cottage. The first thing Shiv saw was the old grandfather clock, with its tick tock, ticking. He noticed that the fireplace was cold and empty now. "It's very quiet Shiv, I don't like it."

"Of course it's quiet, there's no one here but our friends, and they must be sleeping; perhaps they've had a long day too." After a few moments they turned the corner and stepped into the main part kitchen. The cat was fast asleep under the table a just licked clean dish in front of him. "Look Shiv the cushion cat."

"Listen," said the knife, "listen very carefully can you hear?" Stitch leaned his head forward to listen.

"He's snoring; he's fast asleep and snoring."

"Yes" said Shiv, "come on, we have to tip toe past him to reach the dresser."

"But Shiv he's got a licked clean dish, does that mean he's eaten or he's waiting to eat?"

"There's only one way to find out." Shiv and Stitch began to tip toe past the sleeping cat, at one point Twizzle's tail twitched and Stitch almost let out a cry, he would have done if Shiv hadn't put his hand over the needle's mouth. "Sorry Shiv" he whispered, "I thought he was waking up." By the kitchen table the cushion cat's whiskers began to twitch first one then another then another. But Shiv and Stitch had already started the long climb. "Look" whispered Shiv suddenly" the drawer, help me open it come on." The two friends pulled and tugged, tugged and pulled, until finally the old drawer began to slide forward. "Is it wide enough Shiv is it, is it?" they popped their heads over the top of the drawer. "Surprise everybody we're back." The drawer was silent; dusty and empty. Shiv and Stitch clambered inside their happiness suddenly gone as they stood silently for a moment. "Why Shiv, after all we've been through?" Shiv spotted the old label fastened with a drawing pin, they both quickly hurried over, there in Percy's handwriting was a message. Gone to look for Shiv and Stitch, back soon we hope. The two friends slipped down to the floor. "Shiv",

"I know Stitch, I know what you're thinking about, you're worried about our friends and the danger they will be facing you're also thinking about one eye and No Bones and all those horrible weasels, not forgetting of course the pirates and stoats. Come on settle down we need some rest, tomorrows going to be another day. Very, very soon the two friends were fast asleep.

~ ~ ~

Meanwhile from their hiding place on Dragon mills broken sails Captain No-Bones placed the telescope over Ragweed's shoulder, through it he watched as a small band of shiny points made a fire on the edge of Pike wood. "Perfect" hissed the rat just perfect." He closed the telescope and pushed it back into his belt. "All of you hurry we must meet at the old mill wheel, there is much to do."

"Aye, aye Captain No-Bones" There was a movement in the shadows.

"So cousin One Eye, look see how the little fire burns brightly into the night."

"I see it well enough, It's a guide cousin, and will take us straight to their camp."

One Eye the sly and Captain No-Bones laughed, and then disappeared into the shadows.

"It's just the beginning isn't it?" whispered Ragweed to Wrinkle as they waited.

"Yes Ragweed it's just a beginning."

THE END

Zeitfracht Medien GmbH
Ferdinand-Jühlke-Straße 7
99095 Erfurt, Deutschland
produktsicherheit@kolibri360.de

Druck:
CPI Druckdienstleistungen GmbH
im Auftrag der
Zeitfracht Medien GmbH
Ein Unternehmen der Zeitfracht - Gruppe
Ferdinand-Jühlke-Str. 7
99095 Erfurt